A Vampire's Kiss

Also From Rebecca Zanetti

Fallen
Shaken novella
Broken
Driven
Unforgiven

REALM ENFORCERS
Wicked Ride
Wicked Edge
Wicked Burn
Wicked Kiss
Wicked Bite

SCORPIUS SYNDROME SERIES
Scorpius Rising novella
Blaze Erupting novella
Mercury Striking
Shadow Falling
Justice Ascending
Storm Gathering
Winter Igniting
Knight Awakening

SIN BROTHERS
Forgotten Sins
Sweet Revenge
Blind Faith
Total Surrender

BLOOD BROTHERS (Continuation of Sin Brothers)
Deadly Silence
Lethal Lies
Twisted Truths

MAVERICK MONTANA SERIES
Against the Wall
Under the Covers
Rising Assets
Over the Top

A Vampire's Kiss

A Dark Protectors/Rebels Novella

By Rebecca Zanetti

1001 DARK NIGHTS
PRESS

A Vampire's Kiss
A Dark Protectors/Rebels Novella
By Rebecca Zanetti

Copyright 2023 Rebecca Zanetti
ISBN: 979-8-88542-005-1

Foreword: Copyright 2014 M. J. Rose

Published by 1001 Dark Nights Press, an imprint of Evil Eye Concepts, Incorporated

Acknowledgments from the Author

A huge thank you to Liz Berry, MJ Rose, and Jillian Stein for banding together this amazing group of authors who have become such good friends.

Thanks also to the entire 1001 Dark Nights team: Kimberly Guidroz, Chelle Olson, Asha Hossain, Kasi Alexander, Jessica Saunders, and Chris Graham.

Also, thanks to Anissa Beatty and the entire FB Rebecca's Rebels Street Team for the support!

Finally, a huge thank you to my family, Big Tone, Gabe, and Karlina for the support and laughs. I love you three.

One Thousand and One Dark Nights

Once upon a time, in the future...

*I was a student fascinated with stories and learning.
I studied philosophy, poetry, history, the occult, and
the art and science of love and magic. I had a vast
library at my father's home and collected thousands
of volumes of fantastic tales.*

*I learned all about ancient races and bygone
times. About myths and legends and dreams of all
people through the millennium. And the more I read
the stronger my imagination grew until I discovered
that I was able to travel into the stories... to actually
become part of them.*

*I wish I could say that I listened to my teacher
and respected my gift, as I ought to have. If I had, I
would not be telling you this tale now.
But I was foolhardy and confused, showing off
with bravery.*

*One afternoon, curious about the myth of the
Arabian Nights, I traveled back to ancient Persia to
see for myself if it was true that every day Shahryar
(Persian: شهریار, "king") married a new virgin, and then
sent yesterday's wife to be beheaded. It was written
and I had read that by the time he met Scheherazade,
the vizier's daughter, he'd killed one thousand
women.*

Something went wrong with my efforts. I arrived in the midst of the story and somehow exchanged places with Scheherazade – a phenomena that had never occurred before and that still to this day, I cannot explain.

Now I am trapped in that ancient past. I have taken on Scheherazade's life and the only way I can protect myself and stay alive is to do what she did to protect herself and stay alive.

Every night the King calls for me and listens as I spin tales. And when the evening ends and dawn breaks, I stop at a point that leaves him breathless and yearning for more. And so the King spares my life for one more day, so that he might hear the rest of my dark tale.

As soon as I finish a story... I begin a new one... like the one that you, dear reader, have before you now.

Prologue

1849

Dying was just as painful as Ivy had imagined. Her head felt three sizes too small, with a pain that pounded through her ears. She lay on the cot in the old shed, waiting for her time when she could see her mama again. She'd lived nearly twenty-two summers, which was quite a long time for a woman not to get married, but the farm was too far from any village for her to have made any friends. Her father had little use for her other than to upkeep the house and tend the few remaining animals.

She had a gift with them. Even her father could see that, and once he'd even allowed her to visit two farms a distance away that were having problems with their livestock. She'd somehow sensed their illnesses as well as which herbs to include in their feed. The farmers had been so grateful they'd sent her home with enough material to make two dresses.

It was too bad she couldn't save the crops, as well.

The famine was killing all of the small farms.

Somehow, it was her fault he hadn't been granted sons before her mother passed on. There was only Ivy, and when she'd caught the fever, he had brought her to a place housing the sick and left her. At least he'd bothered to cart her into the makeshift hospital where so many were dying. In fact, many of them were put out in wooden sheds, awaiting their turn to go beyond.

She tried to stretch her legs beneath the heavy blanket and winced as the wool rubbed the horrendous rash on her legs. The healer had called the illness typhus, and she supposed something about to kill her should have such a terrifying name.

The hole-riddled door opened, but she didn't bother opening her eyes. She felt the life draining from her, and she was ready. It was time.

A heavy hand descended on her shoulder, and she blinked, looking up, her vision blurry. As such, she could only make out the shapes of two men. She blinked again, trying to focus. "Father?" No, he wouldn't have come to visit her. He had dropped her off and moved on.

"Ivy," he said.

She tried to swallow. That *was* her father. Had he come to witness her death, or did he have a message for her mother? She would be more than happy to take it with her into the beyond.

"You're going to be saved, girl," he said, his voice scratchy.

She must be dreaming. This was one of those visions she kept falling into. Now, she understood. The other form came closer, dropping near her.

"Ivy?"

She tried to make out his features but only saw dark hair and piercing blue eyes. Was he an angel? Perhaps he was ready to take her.

"Yes," she whispered, her voice cracking, and her throat so dry it hurt to even push out that much sound.

"I'm Athan. I'm here to help you." His voice was different, the low tenor difficult to make out. He had an accent that tilted at the ends of the words, and yet the tone was deep. She couldn't comprehend what he was saying. He came closer, and his breath was minty. When was the last time she had smelled something good?

She tried to lean closer to him, but her body had given up the fight and wouldn't move.

"Do you want to live forever?" he asked.

"Yes," she said. Did forever mean dying and going beyond? She would love to see her mother again.

"Say you're sure."

She could barely keep her eyes open. "I'm sure."

"There you go," her father said, his voice booming. "She agreed. You promised you'd save the farm."

"I did," the mysterious Athan said. "But I don't think she's well enough to decide."

Her father sucked in air like he did when about to go into a tantrum. "She's well enough. She's yours now."

Athan leaned closer, his mouth near her ear. "You have to be sure, lass. Is this something you want?"

The question tumbled around in her head. Had her father just given her away in marriage as she was dying? He'd been threatening to do so for years, but she knew he needed help on the farm and would never do so. She'd long ago given up her dreams of having a husband and a family.

"It's too late," she whispered.

"No, it's not. I can save you, but it means you'll be with me forever. Understand?"

None of this made sense, and frankly, she didn't care. This was probably her last dream before dying, so why not entertain the idea? "I would like to live."

"Fair enough," he said. Cool liquid then poured down her throat. There had been water near? She hadn't known. Then something chalky caked at the back of her tongue. Some sort of medicine? She tried to spit it out, and he gently placed his hand over her mouth.

"Swallow the dampening pills. You're not strong enough for anything else."

She obeyed because there was no choice, and this wasn't happening anyway.

Sleep welcomed her with heated arms.

* * * *

One month after escaping death, Ivy fluttered around the opulent sitting room of a brick manor near the center of Belfast. It was fancier than she could've ever imagined, and it was difficult to believe she was still alive. There was nothing to do and nothing to clean. Her strength had returned, her rash had disappeared, and she had plenty of sustenance—unlike many of the people in Ireland.

She wore an elegant gown, soft slippers, and silk undergarments, the likes of which she'd only seen once in a store window. Matching green ribbons tied back her mass of thick hair. While she was clean and pampered, she was rapidly becoming bored.

A knock sounded at her door, and she steeled herself to be examined by her personal nurse again. The woman was brisk but efficient, and she lacked any of the answers Ivy so badly needed. "Enter," she said warily, sitting gracefully on a lovely pink chair.

The door opened, and a man stood there.

Her breath quickened, and she sat straighter, making sure her luxurious skirts were splayed out properly.

He walked inside the room, so tall she had to crane her neck to watch him. His eyes were a piercing blue, his hair raven-black, and his chest broad enough for him to be a bricklayer. There was something familiar about him, but she couldn't place him.

"How are you feeling?" He shut the door behind himself as if he had every right to do so.

She swallowed and tried to speak, but no sound emerged.

This was improper. But his voice... He was from her dream, right before she died.

He stepped closer and then sat in the other chair, his body too big for the carved furniture. Yet his bulk came from muscle rather than fat, much like the wild stallions she'd once seen. "Ivy?"

"You know my name," she whispered.

"Yes." One of his dark eyebrows rose. "What do you remember?" His voice was a low timbre that had the oddest effect on her skin. Goose bumps rose along her arms and over her neck.

She tried to think back. "I was dying, and you were there." At his encouraging nod, she slowly relaxed. "My father was there, and..." She couldn't say the rest. Had her father given her to this stranger? If so, how had he saved her? Many people had succumbed to the fever, and none of them had healed like this—in less than a month. "Who are you?"

He stood and stalked gracefully to a bar area by the door, pouring himself a glass of whisky from a heavy decanter. "Would you like one?"

Ladies didn't drink, at least according to her father. "No, thank you."

He returned to his seat, swirling the dark liquid in the glass. That impossibly blue gaze wandered over her face. "You're quite pretty when not covered with typhus."

How inappropriate for him to remark on her countenance. Unless they were betrothed. Even so, the statement showed a lack of manners. So why had her heart warmed and her body heated? Perhaps she was still ill. She had so many questions, but she'd learned young to bite her tongue and wait for answers. This man was probably much like her father, and his size alone made him a threat. So, she just watched him—and waited.

He took a generous drink of the alcohol. "My name is Athan Maxwell."

His surname was Scottish, but she'd never heard the name Athan before. This was all too befuddling, but she couldn't ask about their status. "My father has not been to visit me."

"No," Athan said. "I told him he wasn't to see you again unless you decided otherwise."

Nobody issued orders to her father. "Why?" She held her breath.

"He gave you to me whether he had a right to do so or not."

Oh. "You must have paid him a tidy sum." She had no illusions about her father's need for her servitude to him and the farm. Yet the potato crop had failed, and the world was starving and ill.

"I did," Athan agreed, his gaze not leaving her. It was relentless.

She shivered and tried to cover the act. "How did you heal me?" Perhaps there was a way to help everyone out of this fever.

Athan held up his right hand to show a truly stunning marking of an M with barbed wire all around it.

"You were branded?" she whispered, shocked.

"Actually, *you* were branded," he said. "I transferred this from my hand to your lower back." His shrug emphasized his broad shoulders. "I figured you'd want to be able to hide the marking beneath clothing."

Marking? Branding? From his hand? "I do not understand."

"I know." Slowly, twin fangs slid down in his mouth.

She gasped, her heart thundering. The legends were true. She'd heard them whispered since she was a tiny girl, but she'd thought they were just fairy tales created to scare children. "You're a vampire."

"I am," he said. "I'm also part demon. Immortals can mate certain humans, and you were one of those. In addition, you were created to be my mate. We just saved each other, beautiful."

Her heart thundered so hard her rib cage hurt. "Am I a vampire?" Oh, no. Had he turned her into someone who drank blood?

"No." He laughed. "You're still human, just enhanced. You'll live forever, but you can only have one mate, and that's me."

She tried to make sense of those words and looked around the lovely room, attempting to focus. "I don't know what that means."

"Somehow, the Maxwell family is cursed. If we don't find our mate by the time we're four centuries old, we die. We start disintegrating before that time and becoming weaker. It's ugly. Imagine an apple losing all of its moisture."

How was that possible? "This affects only your family and not all immortals?"

"Aye," he murmured. "Someday, maybe we'll understand why or how…but not now. Now, we search for our mates, our one and only, and then try to live. But we're always connected at that point. I need you…and you need me."

What was this need of which he spoke? She couldn't bring herself to ask. "How did you find me, if I'm your mate?"

"Luck, fortitude…and fate." He lifted a shoulder—a powerful one. "My grams is a witch, and she has a knack for sending us in the right direction. I believe she uses the elements to do so, but she won't share her secrets. Yet, anyway."

This was too much, but Ivy had always accepted reality. "There's nothing special about me."

"You're quite wrong about that." His gaze wandered over her face. "Immortals can only mate enhanced humans, so you must have an ability. A rare one."

She clasped her hands in her lap. "No. Well, I have a gift with animals, but that's just…"

"Your enhancement." His gaze swept her body. "One of them, anyway."

Her skin tingled, and she straightened. "What does this mating mean for me?"

"It means you can live your life, but we must meet up once a year to exchange blood. It's the only way either of us will survive. I'm sorry you weren't well enough to choose this for yourself, but when it came to it, I saved your life and mine."

She blinked. "Once a year?" What was she to do the rest of the time? "So, we're not married?"

"No, and there can be nobody else for either of us, Ivy. I'll make sure you have a good and very long life."

She sat back in the chair, stunned and feeling more alone than ever. How would she have a good life without a husband and children? "Did we, um, share a marital bed?" She lived on a farm and somewhat understood what that entailed. Shouldn't she feel different?

"No. I bit you and branded you without the marital bed," he drawled. "That might be necessary someday, but apparently not right now since the brand transferred."

It appeared as if he were indifferent to her. Why didn't that grant her relief? They were to remain faithful but apart? What manner of life was that? Would she have to return to the farm? "What about family?" she whispered.

His eyes flared. "Someday, I'll want children, and we'll talk about it then." For the first time, she noticed a scar dissecting the right side of his neck. It was white against his suntanned skin and looked like he'd been slashed with three blades at once. As if catching her gaze, he rubbed the destroyed flesh. "My job is dangerous, and I don't know how long it'll last, so you can't be in my world. It's deadly, and you deserve a bright life and a chance to live it. Even if I don't survive."

She shivered from his matter-of-fact tone. "Why don't you secure a different job?"

His smile was a quick flash of teeth that warmed her in personal places. "There's a threat out there, Ivy, and I hunt threats. I was born and bred to do it. Someday, I hope the danger will be destroyed, but it has to be me." His gaze ran over her face as if he wanted to memorize every angle. "There's a chance I won't survive, and if so, I've cursed you with a very long life alone. I hope that doesn't happen, but at least you'll have a chance now to actually *live*."

The idea that she could not only live but explore her homeland filled her with hope, although she had no means. "Are you sure we're fated?" Her people believed in fate.

"I'm sure," he said, and she had no reason not to believe him. "I'll find you once a year to exchange blood, and at all other times, I promise to keep you as safe as possible from afar. You'll have all the money you need or could want, and your freedom is yours."

It was too much to hope for, but he'd been honest with her so far. A longing filtered through her that they couldn't journey together, but she should be grateful she'd been saved from death. Perhaps she could even live for another ten years or so. It was more than she'd ever dared hope. "I suppose I should return and help my father for a while."

"No. Your father no longer needs help." Athan's tone was gentle, but his gaze was firm. He reached out and untied one of the ribbons from her hair, slipping the pretty silk into his front pocket. "Right now, you need to live your life, and I must go live mine. Pack up, sweetheart. You're sailing to the new world."

Chapter One

Modern Day

This funeral was much more fun than Ivy's last one, which occurred around 1940. The smell of flowers was thick in the air, and it was a delightful gardenia-type scent, unlike the heavy roses from decades ago. All in all, it was a lovely day, considering this was the third time she'd died. She was having a marvelous time.

She tilted her head and studied the picture of her—well, partially of her—from the last few months. She'd posed for it after deliberately caking on all the makeup she'd been wearing in heavier doses for the last several decades. It'd be fun to be herself again, freeing and lighter. So, she stood near the coffin and took note that next time she aged, she'd have to use a lighter touch around her eyes. She didn't look quite right in the photograph.

A figure stepped up to her side. "She was truly a lovely woman."

Ivy looked sideways at Herman Jones, the forty-year-old snake who'd tried to steal the company out from under her. Her business increasing the longevity of cattle had expanded into several specialty animal organizations catering to people who needed service animals. She'd miss working with the dogs but would most certainly use her enhancement, one that discovered what animals needed, in another arena. "Herman, how nice to meet you." It was a good thing she'd had everybody wear name tags. Otherwise, she couldn't pretend not to know them. She held out a hand.

"Oh. No. It's nice to meet you, and I'm so sorry it's under such terrible circumstances." Herman bent over her hand and brushed his lips across her knuckles. She withdrew quickly, knowing the rash that could occur from having another male touch her.

When she'd mated Athan, or at least when he'd mated her, a reaction had started in her body that prevented any other male from touching her. He hadn't explained that back in the day, but then again, he hadn't explained much, now, had he?

Herman leaned closer. "Your aunt said so many lovely things about you. I apologize for not meeting you before now."

Considering it was impossible for her to be in two places at once, there was no way she could have met him. Plus, the guy was a jerk. "You know my aunt spoke very fondly of you," she lied, rather enjoying the game.

He nodded somberly and glanced at the solid gold watch on his wrist. "That was kind of her. I don't mean to be indelicate, but..."

Ivy almost burst out laughing. Instead, she let her lips tremble as if she were genuinely overcome by emotion. "But what?"

Herman cleared his throat. "It's my understanding that the outstanding stock certificates for the company haven't been accounted for as yet."

She drew in air and let the moment stretch, trying really hard not to smile. Finally, she patted his sleeve, careful not to touch his skin. "Oh. I'm sorry about that mix-up, but no. She sold the company." To a wonderful, dog-loving couple out of Omaha who owned several cattle ranches.

Herman reared back, his eyes a stormy blue, and his perfectly styled grayish-brown hair swept back from his face. "Excuse me?"

"Oh. Yes," Ivy said. "She sold about a month ago to Tandem Enterprises out of Nebraska. I'm surprised she didn't tell you." In fact, Ivy hadn't told anybody because she'd wanted to enjoy this moment. Of course, she'd had to sell the company. She needed the funds for her new enterprise—well, the startup she'd begun months ago as her current self. It felt so good to go without tons of aging makeup and gray powder in her hair, and now she could finally make a difference.

Herman's face turned a mottled red. "This is unacceptable."

Featherlight, a figure stepped up to Ivy's other side. "Oh, Ivy. I'm so sorry. How are things going?" Leah asked, her eyelashes fluttering.

Ivy patted her arm and dug in her nails. "Just lovely, Leah. Thank you for asking." It was fun to use their original names again since they hadn't done so in nearly a century.

Leah reached beyond Ivy and held out a hand. "We haven't met. You seem upset."

Herman shook her hand, and Leah drew back as quickly as she could.

Ivy glanced down to see a rash forming on Leah's thumb and hand. Served her right. She shouldn't have jumped in, but Leah didn't know any other way.

Herman smiled. "Leah. You were friends with Ms. Masters?"

"Yes," Leah said. "We engaged in several business enterprises together. She was quite brilliant, you know."

Herman nodded, his eyes warming. "I do know, and she did rely on me quite a bit. In fact, it looks like I'm out of a job now that she has passed on. You wouldn't need a head of accountancy in any of your, um, enterprises, would you?"

Leah fluttered her hands. "No. I'm sorry. My company's fully employed right now, but it's still kind of you to offer." She linked her arm through Ivy's and pulled her away to sit in the front pew as the funeral began and people spoke eloquently about who Ivy had been. It was nice to hear that her efforts had paid off, and the many charities she'd supported through her businesses had made good use of the funds.

Too many people had nice stories about her, and she soon started to drift away. Where was Athan today? She flashed back to a time in the early 1920s when he'd unexpectedly shown up at her flat.

The knock at the door surprised her, considering it was late, so she hustled to open it. She was up reading the newest projections for the stocks she'd just purchased under one of her assumed names. It was surprising how much talent she'd discovered in her ability to project winners. There was no danger in opening her door at midnight. Her penthouse was well protected by doormen and security throughout the building, so only a friend could even reach her doorway.

Athan sagged to the side, his shirt and trousers in tatters and blood pouring from several wounds. "Ivy," he whispered, his eyes showing bizarre gold spikes through the blue.

She pulled him inside, her heart thundering. Without being asked, she lifted her wrist to his mouth.

His fangs instantly pierced her flesh, and he started drinking. A feeling she'd learned to identify as desire swept through her, swishing along her skin and digging deeply into her body. As she watched, the wounds on his neck and chest closed, the skin stitching together smoothly. He slowly withdrew the pearly points from her and licked her wrist clean.

She shuddered, feeling like his tongue was everywhere.

He leaned back, his eyes their shearing blue again. Then he kissed her.

Shock immobilized her for two seconds, and then she sank into the devastating sensations. Growling, he wrapped an arm around her waist and drew her against his hard body. They'd met once a year for decades, and this was the first time he'd kissed her.

It was heaven.

Finally, he released her and pulled away.

She blinked, touching her tingling lips. That was so much. "Are you finished with your hunting job?" she whispered.

He blinked. "No."

Disappointment crashed through her, but she struggled to smile. He'd promised her life and had given it to her. She shouldn't want for more and should be grateful. Even though she was finding her own way in life, she sometimes still felt beholden to him. Yet the more she learned and lived, the more she felt a spirit of independence awakening inside her. "What is this hunting job, Athan?" He never wanted to talk about it, but she deserved some answers.

He sighed. "There are more than vampires out there, darlin'. Our enemy, the Kurjans, have been creating werewolves out of shifters."

Shifters? "Excuse me?"

"Shifters can change from human form to animal, and they're our allies—well, usually." He pulled off his destroyed shirt to reveal a broad and muscular chest.

Her lungs stuttered, and heat flared in her face. "They become animals?"

"Yes. But werewolves are pure animal—no humanity and no conscience. We've hunted them for centuries because Maxwells have an instinct for them, which doesn't speak well of us. But we're the best at hunting and killing them." He reached out and ran his thumb along her jawline. "The Kurjans are trying to create the monsters in a quantity that could harm the population on this planet."

On this planet? Were there others? "I don't understand."

"I know." His hand dropped, and her skin felt chilled. "It's hard to explain, but three prison worlds were created far away from this one, and that imbalance has allowed more werewolves to be born and bred. Until those worlds fall, and this one gets back in alignment, I hunt killers every day."

None of that made a bit of sense, but she believed him. "Perhaps you need somebody by your side," she murmured, wanting to ease his torment.

He leaned over and kissed her gently on the nose. "Anybody by my side gets bloody and most likely dead. I appreciate the offer, and I admire your kind spirit. But this is just a short stopover before my next fight." He leaned away, taking his warmth with him. "I am getting weaker, though. We'll need to meet twice a year now."

It was embarrassing how much pleasure that thought gave her. Twice a year?

She'd never admit it, but she lived for these moments of brief intimacy. It was sad, actually.

Leah jerked Ivy back to the present and pulled her to stand. "Everyone is done and clearing out. Are we finished admiring what's left of your life here?" she muttered.

Ivy shushed her and turned to walk down the center aisle, leaving the intricate urn behind. Somebody was supposed to bury it the next day, but she was finished with this life. "Knock it off. This is fun. We spent all day at your funeral, if I remember right."

Leah nodded. "True, but at least I had a full band so people could dance." For a moment, she lost the gaiety always present in her eyes. "It's hard to see everybody we know die. Right?"

Ivy nodded. "Yeah, but at least this time, I waited to pass on until all my friends had. It was nice growing old with them…well, kind of." She'd only pretended to grow old when they truly had. If nothing else, she'd always have Leah, who was also mated to one of the Maxwell jackasses but somehow seemed to stay off their radar. Ivy usually kept Athan informed of her whereabouts. However, she was keeping her new venture under wraps, and another deadline loomed.

Several people stopped her to express their condolences.

Leah let out a fake sob.

Ivy barely kept from rolling her eyes. "I'm not surprised to see you here, Leah, but we have to be more careful." They had strict instructions to stay away from each other because the last thing they wanted to do was bring notice to any Maxwell mates. There were enemies out there who would like nothing more than getting their hands on either of the women.

Leah shrugged. "Eh. We can handle it. It's not like we haven't spent the last century learning to fight."

Actually, Leah was a pretty good fighter. Ivy had never mastered the movements necessary to really inflict damage on somebody. She didn't have Leah's grace, but she had a darn good brain, and she knew this was stupid. "Let's go. We can grab dinner and then fly to Buffalo."

Truth be told, she would miss California—or perhaps she wouldn't. The crime had gotten ridiculous, and the cost of living was astronomical. She was quite looking forward to relocating to Nashville after they'd finished the op in Buffalo. It was a much friendlier business town; plus, she loved music. It would be lovely to be surrounded by it again as she and Leah finally started making a difference and taking some chances. She was ready.

Leah leaned closer. "So, after we enjoy the lives we just set up for maybe a hundred years, where should we go? I think it's time we left this continent and went to another one."

Ivy nodded. She'd been thinking the same thing. Maybe she'd live one more lifetime in the States and then go somewhere else with a new identity. "We have a lot of good to do first." So long as the Maxwell family didn't discover they were taking chances and working together. The risk was well worth it, though.

A chill skittered down her spine as they walked out into a heated day. Almost on instinct, she turned toward the other side of the street to see a tall and broad figure lounging against a light post, his gaze blue and piercing.

"Whoa," Leah breathed. "Guess your mate came to your funeral."

Chapter Two

Athan Maxwell watched as his wayward mate sashayed out of her own funeral wearing an adorable tight black dress with a sassy black hat partially covering her long, reddish-blond hair. Even across the distance, he saw the crystal-clear green of her eyes. Once again, the sight of her jolted him, landing hard in his solar plexus. She'd only become lovelier through the years as she gained both her independence and a startling penchant for finding trouble.

She appeared nearly brilliant in business, but she took chances in her personal life that he couldn't allow any longer. The enemy drew near, and while he'd tried to protect her for the last century and a half, it was time for her to take precautions. He rubbed the green ribbon in his pocket as he mulled over the situation.

His gaze caught on the woman next to her, and he frowned. Wait a minute. Was that...? He straightened, pushing away from the street light.

Leah Ferry took one look at him, leaned up, whispered something to Ivy, and turned to hustle down the road. He moved to intercept her when she jumped into a waiting black Town Car. The vehicle immediately sped away from the curb and him. He lowered his chin, irritation crackling down his spine. Pausing to make sure no cars flattened him, he strode across the street while pulling his phone from his back pocket and making a quick call.

"Hey, brother," Jasper answered. "What's going on? Did you find him?"

"Not yet," Athan said grimly. The Kurjan scientist who'd just figured out how to mass produce the virus that turned shifters into werewolves was more difficult to draw out than he'd anticipated, but he was on the scent and would find the asshole before plans got put into motion. "But I did find your mate."

Silence pounded across the line for a moment. "Where are you? I thought you were going to Los Angeles."

"I am in LA. Apparently, your mate attended my mate's funeral. They walked out arm in arm." He wasn't a male who let his temper take control very often, and he fought it with both hands right now.

"Are you kidding me?" Jasper asked slowly. "They know to stay away from each other. They know to keep a low profile."

"Apparently, we haven't made that clear enough," Athan said quietly. "She sped off in a Town Car headed east. That's all I know, but I'll get more information for you later."

"Thanks. I'm on it," Jasper said curtly, ending the call.

Athan reached Ivy and looked down at her upturned face. She was far from the meek and bewildered farm girl he'd once known. She stood tall and proud and faced him directly, even though she was still a good foot shorter than he. "Sorry for your loss," he drawled.

Her smile was quick, and her chin lifted. "Well, we can't live forever now can we, mate?" She looked around the busy street. "You're about two months early. We went from once a year to twice, and then every quarter. Yet here you are, early. You want to explain that?"

No. He most certainly did not want to explain that. He was getting weaker, and their enemy was getting stronger. But he couldn't tell her that—or rather, he didn't want to. "I was in town," he lied.

She arched one eyebrow, giving her a pixie-like look instead of a dangerous one. "You just happened to be in LA for my funeral? Why do I find that hard to believe?"

He had to admire her. A hundred years ago, she wouldn't have dared to ask the question. Now, she asked it almost casually as if she didn't actually care about the answer. He'd given her freedom these many decades, and for the first time, he wondered if that had been a wise choice.

He grasped her arm and drew her toward the car he had waiting near the curb. At just that one touch, electricity jolted through him, lancing through his body and sparking him wide awake. He stood straighter, feeling better than he had in months. Just being near her helped fight the curse inside him. "Apparently, we need to talk," he said, ushering her toward the vehicle.

"I'm good," she said, pulling her arm free.

"Actually, you're not." Without waiting for her agreement, he lifted her, tucked them both into the back of the car, and gave the driver an order to go.

She sat in his lap, surprise tilting her face. Then she shoved him hard and moved to the adjoining seat. He allowed her freedom this time. She crossed her arms. "Don't you go ruining my very perfectly nice funeral, Athan Maxwell."

The absurdity of her statement caught him unaware. Amusement bubbled up and through him, battling the possessive lust that only got stronger every time he was around her. "You know you can't take chances like that, right?"

She shrugged and rolled her eyes.

While he had told her about the dangers to them throughout the years, he had never shown her. That was on him, not her.

She looked him over, facing him squarely, her gaze running down his form. "It's only been three months. You look thinner. Are you?"

Yeah, he was thinner. This was getting more and more difficult, and he didn't know how to explain it to her. "No. I'm fine. We need to talk about Leah. Why were you two together?"

Ivy crossed her arms. "That's none of your business."

"Ah, mate," he drawled. "That's exactly where you're wrong. Everything about you is my business, and it appears I've allowed you too much freedom throughout the years. That just changed."

* * * *

"That just changed?" Ivy tilted her head. "Are you threatening me?"

Athan studied her. "I don't believe so." He rubbed the scruff on his sculpted jaw. "If I were threatening you, you would know it."

"Huh," she said. "Interesting." She glanced at her watch, feigning boredom. Every time she was near him, her entire body jolted with electricity, and it only got worse through the years. She couldn't see him more than a couple of times a year or it was just too much. "I think we should go back to twice a year," she murmured.

"Not going to happen," he retorted.

She looked up, startled. In their long time together, he'd never once refused her anything. Irritation smashed through her at the thought that she had to ask him for anything. "I suppose I wasn't clear enough," she murmured. "We are only going to meet twice a year."

One of his dark eyebrows rose. "Ivy, you've had a good life. Well, two actually because I allowed it. For you to think otherwise would be a mistake."

Fire flashed through her on the heels of a temper she very rarely let loose. "Allowed it? Oh, I don't think so, biting boy." By the narrowing of his eyes, he didn't like the nickname. She couldn't blame him. It wasn't very nice. Yet this showdown had been coming for quite a while, and she was ready. "I've made my own money, and I've succeeded in my lives. The time for you telling me what to do is long past. I hope you understand that."

His expression didn't change. "If I don't?"

She thought about it. She really did. "As I see it, Athan, at this point in our lives, you need me a lot more than I need you." It was true, but she had to be fair. "I told you once, and I'll tell you again, I am fine repaying not only the money you gave to my father but also the funds you supplied me with early on in my journey. I'll even pay you interest."

If a vampire could emote anger, this one did. Yet he hadn't moved, and his expression hadn't changed. It was impressive, really, and a skill Ivy wished she could learn. But every emotion she had was still visible on her face, and she knew it. Right now, she was feeling both irritated and angry.

"Ivy, you'll want to stop pushing me. Now," he said softly. Way too softly.

She shivered and quickly covered the movement by leaning back in the seat and crossing her legs. Even though he looked thinner than he had a few months ago, he was still big and broad and probably the most dangerous thing in Los Angeles. His eyes were bluer than ever, his hair just as dark, and his shoulders nearly as wide. There was no doubt he could take out any threat coming for him. While she'd once appreciated that, he was just irritating her now.

"Athan, I'm not kidding. This isn't working for me any longer." He blinked. She sighed. "I know, I owe you my life, and I know I'd be dead and wouldn't be living these wonderful experiences without you. That's why I've continued meeting you through the years. But there has to be something more out there." She'd been feeling it lately. Lonely. She was probably the world's oldest virgin, considering she was nearly one hundred and sixty.

"What are you asking?" he murmured, looking svelte and in control in his dark slacks and white button-down shirt.

Her body heated, a slow roll moving through her. "I'm not asking for anything. I'm just telling you there are rumors."

He stilled without moving. He had the oddest way of controlling the environment around him. "Rumors?"

She finally looked down, unable to keep his gaze. "Yes. I've heard the queen, the one of the Realm, has discovered a virus that negates a mating bond." Her voice trembled, and she cleared her throat, surprised by how much she still wanted to make him happy. She *did* owe him her life.

"No," he said.

She jerked, her head coming up. "Excuse me?" Ah, there was her CEO voice. She'd finally found it.

"I said no."

She shook her head, leaning back and trying to focus on his words instead of letting the roaring through her head overcome her good judgment. "I wasn't asking, Athan." True anger, raw and real, began coursing through her veins.

Through the years, all he'd told her was that they had to exchange blood to survive. Yet she felt fine, and he was weakened, so it appeared that *he* needed *her* blood. She'd studied enough genetics and chromosomal abnormalities to understand there was something within the Maxwell line that required blood from a mate, whereas most vampires and demons didn't need blood. She and Leah had figured that out on their own.

"Why me?" she asked.

He reached out and tapped something on the window separating them from the driver. Some sort of command given in code. "I don't know," he admitted.

Well, that kind of hurt. She didn't know why, but it stung. "What do you mean you don't know?"

"We don't know. Maxwells have, as far as we know, one mate only that can save us from the curse of death. I don't know if it's genetics, fate, or a combination, Ivy, but you're it for me. I know it, and I think you know it, too."

He'd only kissed her three times throughout the years. She wasn't ugly. She knew it. She might not be movie-star glamorous, but she was decent to look at. "Don't you want sex?" she asked.

Finally, an expression filtered through his eyes. It was all flash and heat and gone as quickly as it had arrived. Every nerve she had jumped around in her body, landing low in her abdomen. Warning hissed through her, and she stilled out of instinct.

"Are you asking for sex, darlin'?" he asked, his slight Scottish brogue melding with what sounded like a place where cowboys lived. Was he now a cowboy?

"No." She tossed her head. She might be the world's longest-living virgin, but there was no way she'd beg any man for sex, even the only one who could give it to her. "Of course, not." And yet, curiosity had always been her bane. "But I have to ask, don't you miss it?" She couldn't imagine that he'd been a virgin for the hundred and fifty years he'd lived before he found her.

"Of course, I miss sex," he said, pinching the bridge of his nose as if he were getting a headache.

"Then why? Why have you never made a move?" She liked recent vernacular and was more than happy to use it.

He looked at her then, his gaze blazing, tension rolling off him in fiery-hot waves and heating the car's interior. "Because you didn't have a choice in becoming my mate."

She paused. All these years, she'd thought he wasn't interested. She hadn't given any consideration to any other reasons. "You saved my life."

"Again, you didn't have a choice in that," he admitted. "And you were young, scared, and fresh. You needed to live your life and discover your strength."

She'd appreciated not only the freedom but also the financial support to explore. However, she could support herself now, and she was ready to actually live. "Why are you here, Athan?" she asked. "Why, really?"

He sighed. "I need blood, Ivy, and per our agreement, you're going to give it to me."

Her head shot up, and she opened her mouth to say something, anything that would teach him that she was no longer his to play with. She had her own mind and life, and she either wanted to know everything or she wanted out.

Just then, an explosion rocked the car, and they flew into the air. Her head hit the roof, and sparks blazed through her skull. Then...nothing.

Chapter Three

Glass sliced into Athan's face, and he pivoted instantly to take Ivy down to the floor of the car. She'd hit her head already and wasn't moving. Fury lanced through him. He lifted his head, barking out orders for his younger brother, Klyde, who was driving the vehicle. A series of bullets impacted the glass, and Klyde fell sideways with the car careening toward what looked like a coffee shop.

Growling, Athan jumped up and leaped through the partition between the front and back seats as glass sliced his neck. He landed in the front seat and pivoted, shoving Klyde out of the way so he could grab the wheel and yank it to the side to avoid hitting two women who were scrambling to get away from their table.

Back on the road, he drove rapidly, trying to find the enemy's location. They weren't above him, so they must have been on the sidewalk, which meant he could outrun them. He careened around a corner while pulling his phone from his back pocket and punching the gas. Tersely, he barked orders to any of his men in the area, still searching for the enemy.

Two motorcycles rode up behind him, and both riders started firing green lasers—immortal weapons that'd turn into raw steel the instant they hit flesh.

He glanced behind himself to make sure Ivy was still down. She wasn't moving, but at least she was out of the line of fire. So, he concentrated fully on the two enemies and their supercharged bikes. They were on unmarked black motorcycles with helmets, and both looked tall and broad, though he couldn't determine their species. A minivan and

Town Car were in front of him, so he let them slow him down enough.

The guy on the left quickly approached, and Athan spun around and nicked him with his back bumper. The attacker flew off the motorcycle and through the window of what looked like a shoe store.

Athan spun around a corner to see two of his soldiers careening his way, both on bikes. The only way to handle Los Angeles traffic was on motorcycles. He spun again and let the men ride past him and take over, driving rapidly north and then backtracking several times before barreling into an underground parking garage. The door immediately shut after him, and he screeched to a halt near the elevator.

Klyde moaned next to him and then shook his head, sitting up. Blood cascaded down his face, and he prodded his cheekbone, which had a bone sticking out. "I think I was shot."

"I think you were, too," Athan said, nearly ripping open the back door to reach for Ivy.

She still wasn't moving. He gently pulled her out and checked her for injuries. She wasn't cut, but she was bruised and had a lump the size of an egg on her forehead. He cradled her gently and ran to the elevator with Klyde stumbling along behind him.

"Did you see who it was?" Klyde gasped, leaning over and sucking in air. He had the Maxwell dark hair, but his eyes were a light tawny brown. Normally. Right now, they were a furious silver.

"No. Could have been anybody," Athan muttered, the adrenaline still shooting through his veins.

"Yeah, right," Klyde said.

Athan nodded. "I know, but it could be. I don't know who it was. Hopefully, we caught at least one of them." At the moment, he'd like nothing more than to interrogate whoever had shot at them.

He punched the button for the penthouse, and they rose to the top of the building that mainly housed high-end executives who worked in Hollywood. The penthouse was his and used exclusively for surveillance. He bypassed the living quarters for the main control room, where his people were already scrambling to bring up CCTV footage from the entire area. They would find out who these guys were, trace them back to the source, and then Athan would finally go to war.

He gently laid Ivy on a leather sofa that had been pushed to the far right. Two chairs and a coffee table littered with soda and water bottles flanked the couch. His men had been at it all night since he was in town, surveilling the entire area. It was shocking they hadn't seen the two motorcycle assassins coming, and he wanted to know why.

But first, he crouched and smoothed Ivy's strawberry-blond hair away from her pale face. Her lashes were startlingly dark, considering her pale coloring. A light smattering of freckles dotted her pert nose. Reaching out since she was still unconscious, he gently ran his knuckles along her smooth skin. "Ivy, wake up now, sweetheart."

She didn't stir. He looked again at the lump on her head. It seemed to be going down in size. She was immortal like him, so this wouldn't last long, but she was out for the duration. He looked around for a blanket to cover her, but the control room had none.

He checked her skin, and she felt warm enough. Without being able to help himself, he leaned over and kissed her forehead, making sure the ribbon was still in his pocket like always.

Shoving any and all emotions away, he stood and headed for the nearest console, his gaze on the wide screen on the wall showing the greater downtown Los Angeles area. "Let's find these assholes."

* * * *

Pain flared inside Ivy's head, and she gingerly reached up to feel a lump near her left temple. It was comparable to the time she'd been hit with a cricket bat during what could only be termed an unladylike brawl on the grass. It had been during her last lifetime, but she remembered it well. The pain had taken almost a day to go away. This was similar.

She kept her eyes closed because she knew if she opened them, she'd probably shriek from agony, and she wasn't quite sure where she was yet. She'd learned during her long life to remain still and quiet until she understood fully what was happening.

Activity and men's voices wafted around her, but she couldn't quite make out individual words yet. The roaring between her ears kept her from understanding. So, she patiently waited, noting that she was lying on something smooth and comfortable like a leather couch. Interesting.

Memories came rushing back of the attack in the car and her hitting her head. Somebody had attacked them. Oh, no. Was Athan all right?

She opened her eyes slowly, and lights spiked into them, but she was able to remain still without heaving. Her stomach clenched, but even so, she swallowed several times to regain her bearings. Her throat hurt, and her body felt like one big bruise. She'd never gained the ability to heal herself from injuries like other immortals, so she figured it was because she wasn't truly mated—not in every sense of the word, anyway. But she was immortal, and she'd be okay, even though the pain was pretty intense.

Slowly, figures began taking shape in front of her, and her gaze immediately landed on Athan. He stood in front of a wide screen that showed downtown LA. She knew the area well.

Even though soldiers bustled around, rapidly handing each other notes and maps, typing, or barking orders into phones, there was no doubt who was in command. There was almost a force field around him that vibrated with tension and anger. Even in profile, she could see that his eyes had turned a deep midnight color with gold rims and sparks. They were his tertiary vampire colors, and she'd only seen them twice in their entire long lives together.

One time, she'd thought it had been desire that'd brought those colors forth when he'd been feeding from her, and the atmosphere had changed around them—to something new. But right now, there was no doubt it was rage. He held still as if in control, but anger and fury popped the oxygen around him. There was no doubt that Athan Maxwell didn't like being caught by surprise.

A soldier from across the room looked up from his computer. "Athan, I have the video from this morning. There were no tails on Ivy from the time she left her penthouse to the time you fetched her at the funeral."

Fetched? Did he say *fetched*? Like she was some sort of pet? Ivy barely kept from sitting up, but she remained in place, wanting to know more. They'd probably stop speaking if they realized she was awake.

"Show me," Athan ordered. A video came up on the screen of Ivy exiting the penthouse, walking down her hall, taking the elevator, and then emerging to where her driver awaited in front of the building she still owned.

The soldier in the far corner, one who looked suspiciously like Athan, aimed a laser pointer at the screen to show two people sitting on either side of the street outside her place, one waiting for a bus, and then one lounging against a tree. "Here's the detail we had in place, and they'd been stationed there for two hours. Nobody approached the building, and there's no hint of electrical surveillance anywhere near."

Ivy barely kept from gasping.

"Show me the rest of the day," Athan ordered.

Surreally, Ivy's entire day showed on the screen—from when she arrived at the funeral and everything she did there, up until she met

Athan. No moment of her day was unaccounted for. Did they have cameras in her penthouse, as well? Shock and betrayal poured through her.

"Pause," Athan ordered when Ivy and Leah strode out of the building. "Klyde? You're on Leah. Find out where she came from and where she went. Our older brother will very much appreciate it."

So it was true. Leah had managed to evade Jasper all these years. Ivy bit her lip. Had her friendship put Leah in danger? She leaned to the side to check out Klyde, the youngest of the Maxwell brothers. She'd never met him, but Athan had told her all about his brothers through the years. Klyde had longish black hair, mellow brown eyes, and a broad chest.

"Good," Athan muttered. "Show me the rest of the day."

The video rolled with Ivy looking rather carefree, considering she'd just attended her own funeral. From this birds-eye view, she started to make out the surveillance teams that had been all around her when she'd had absolutely no clue.

All these years, thinking she'd been independent and building her different lives, and he'd been watching? Not only had he been watching, he'd had people on her the entire time. She sat up fully then, her head spinning not only from the goose egg on her temple but also from chilled shock.

Had her freedom just been an illusion all these decades? Fury clicked through her so quickly her hands shook. For a second, she couldn't breathe. The roaring in her ears grew louder. So far, nobody had noticed her movements.

Athan glanced over his other shoulder at the guy at the keyboard. "I want to see her entire week before this. I want to make sure that whoever attacked was aiming for me and not her."

Leon shook his head. "If I wanted to attack her, I would've stayed under the radar and waited for her funeral. It was in the news, and she wouldn't have been that difficult to link to you, brother." He winced. "Sorry."

Athan's jaw hardened. "Show me her week anyway."

Her entire week? She wanted to shake her head, but she didn't want to face the ensuing pain. Even so, her heart started beating so fast her ribs hurt. How could he? How could he lie to her all these years? How could he make her think she was an independent woman, growing her life and businesses? Was any of it true? Had he interfered with all of it? She stood and wobbled slightly before planting her feet.

He slowly turned his head toward her, his eyes still those devastating and deadly colors. "Ivy, how's your head?"

She clenched her fingers into fists. For a moment, her throat was too hot to speak. She swallowed several times and lowered her chin, her voice shaking. "You fucking bastard."

Chapter Four

Athan didn't allow himself to outwardly react and instead studied his mate. She stood with her legs braced in her four-inch black heels with their red soles, looking both furious and sexy in her formfitting funeral dress. Her strawberry-blond hair cascaded down her back, and the lump on her forehead, while still visible, seemed to be decreasing in size even more. Her eyes spit green fire, and a lovely Irish rose color had flushed her cheeks.

While she was truly the most gorgeous thing he'd ever seen, he probably couldn't let her get away with calling him a bastard.

It was the first time in nearly a century and a half that he'd heard her swear. For some reason, it intrigued him more than it angered him. Even so, the words didn't sound natural coming from her sweet mouth.

He rubbed his jaw and mulled over the situation, noting he hadn't shaved in a few days. "How is your temple?"

If anything, his question seemed to infuriate her further. Her body vibrated, and her little hands clenched into tight fists. He had no doubt she'd punch him if he were within striking range. For some inexplicable reason, that did nothing but arouse him. The anger he'd been feeling about the attack earlier was quickly morphing into something else, something neither of them needed right now, especially since he was hunting a psychopathic Kurjan doctor who'd most likely just tried to kill him. Oh, it was the long game, and he had a lot of time left in this hunt, but apparently, he and his brothers were getting closer.

The entire room had gone quiet around them, but he cared little what anybody else thought. His focus was centered on the woman who seemed to be battling a temper he hadn't realized she had. Fascinating.

He didn't look away from her as he issued orders to his soldiers. "Bring up video from the entire week and then bring up my timeline. Let's find out where these guys caught wind of us. Ivy, we'll go talk." He started to move toward her.

If anything, she settled her stance firmer. "I'm not going anywhere with you, dick—"

He cut her off before she could finish the sentence, ducking his head and tossing her over one shoulder. With smooth strides, he continued out of the control room with her struggling and fighting him, to little avail. While he'd given her immortality, there was no way to give her additional strength or speed. He planted an arm over her legs to keep her from kicking him in the stomach again and continued through the door and down the hallway to the living quarters. It had been a while since he'd stayed here, and even then, it had been to recuperate from a fight. He'd felt her near several times but hadn't called on her. Through the years, he'd tried not to demand her blood outside of their schedule, which was now four times a year unless he was in dire need.

It was becoming too difficult to stay away from her. Every time they touched, he wanted to make her fully his, which wasn't fair since he still faced death daily. But having her squirming body over his shoulder set his blood pounding with demand throughout his entire being. This wasn't safe for either of them.

The words she spat at him were quite an intriguing combination of curses and threats. A few were combined in a way he hadn't heard in his long lifetime. Even as she punched him squarely in the kidneys, he fought his grin. She couldn't do any damage, but she was trying her hardest.

Kicking the door shut behind him, he flipped her over and planted her in a chair in a nicely appointed living room. The bedroom was to the left, and he purposefully didn't look that way. Right now, he had to keep both of them in check, and she was doing her best to make sure that didn't happen.

She bunched her legs to bound out of the chair, and he planted one hand on her shoulder, easily forcing her to remain in place. "You sit and knock it off. I've had about enough of this."

She growled then. It wasn't quite a vampire-demon growl, but it sure as shit was rather impressive. "You ass—"

"Stop," he snapped, putting command in his voice this time. "That's the third time you've called me a name in less than a minute, and I'm done with it. If you want to talk about this, we can do so. If you wish to continue acting the brat, you'll be treated as such." Her defiance was doing nothing but turning him on, and he needed to get control of the situation—and them—before he lost all his good intentions.

She instantly turned and sank her teeth into his hand.

Pain flashed through his skin, and he jerked, startled. Blood welled from the flesh between his thumb and index finger, and he looked at it, bemused. "You just bit me."

She moved to stand, and this time he let her. "Get out of my way, Athan." She shoved him in the abs, digging her fingers between them.

Oh, that was it. He let his fangs drop. "You want to bite, sweetheart? I bite back." The marking on his palm heated and flared as if demanding that he finally plant it on her completely. She'd admitted that the marking had faded through the years, but he hadn't seen it for himself. However, the marking on his hand had slowly darkened, so it made sense.

She tried to take a step away, but the chair hampered her movements. She held out both hands to push him again, but her palms didn't make contact. He smoothly manacled both her wrists together and jerked her toward him, leaning down until his nose almost touched hers. "You about done with this defiance?"

She tossed her head, and her nostrils flared. "Not even close." She kicked him square in the ankle then, the sharp point of her fancy shoe nicking him right between bone and flesh.

At her show of temper, his calmed. One of them had to be in control, and it was most definitely him right now. "Oh, sweetheart," he said, "that's it." He fell back onto the matching chair, pulling her with him. While anger had nearly ruled him earlier, logic and determination took hold now. In one smooth movement, he pulled her to the side and down, flattening her over his thighs.

Her startled yelp pleased him much more than it should have.

The woman had a delightful ass that had haunted his dreams more than once over the years. In the formfitting dress, the twin globes all but tempted him to bite her and leave his mark on her butt. Instead, he lifted one hand and let it descend with a loud smack that echoed around the peaceful suite.

She gasped, stiffened, and then began to struggle in earnest. "You son of a—"

Smack.

"Why, you jack—"

Smack.

She paused in her tirade, stilling. "Athan, let me up." Her hair fell forward to shield her face, and her voice was muffled.

The woman apparently didn't understand the lesson yet, but at least she had stopped calling him names. "No. Apologize nicely to me for biting, kicking, and insulting me," he said, spreading his left hand over her entire lower back to hold her in place. His right hand itched to smack her perfect ass again.

She managed to be quiet for almost two seconds. "No. You are a complete jerk, and—"

Smack, smack, smack. He brought his hand down in rapid succession with just enough force to jolt her but not enough to actually hurt her. They'd been mated for well over a century, and apparently, he hadn't been paying close enough attention to her if she thought she could physically assault him with no repercussions. If she thought she could get away with such disrespect, which didn't matter in the grand scheme of things, then she might believe she could disobey him in more important issues such as safety and subterfuge, which absolutely *did* matter. She could get them both killed. "I can do this all day, sweetheart," he murmured, flattening his right hand over her ass and feeling the heat. "Apologize."

She struggled again, and he had to admire her grit. A lot.

Even so, he smacked her once more. Harder. "Apologize, Ivy." The fact that she and Leah had been meeting showed she was no longer afraid of him or his rules, and that was a good thing. The girl who'd feared him was gone, and a courageous woman remained in her place—one he'd patiently waited for through the eons. While he didn't want her fear, he did need her respect. Or at least enough of it that she'd stay safe and not put herself in danger like she had. This lesson mattered, and they'd stay until she learned it. "Ivy," he warned.

She tried to kick out and wriggle off his thighs, but her strength was no match for his. "You'll pay for this," she yelled, reaching for his ankle to dig in her nails. They were sharp and drew blood. "I mean it. You'll regret this in ways your moronic brain can't even compute right now. You don't want me for an enemy."

Probably. He did love a good threat, and she seemed determined. But safety mattered, and the woman needed to listen to him now more than ever. She had to understand repercussions, and he had no doubt he'd have to reinforce this lesson soon. Right now, they were running out of time. He could feel the fight inside her, so he made it easier for her to submit by increasing the power in his slaps until she squirmed and then yelped.

"Fine," she spat. "I apologize."

There was no doubt she didn't mean it, and if they were truly mated, he'd take her to the point where she truly submitted. But he didn't have that right, nor did he have the time, considering somebody was trying to kill one or both of them with modern weapons. Plus, he had no illusions of where that lesson would lead, and once he finally took her to bed, he wanted all the time in the world to explore her.

So, he lifted her off his lap, standing her between his knees until she regained her footing. She balanced herself with her hands on his thighs and then drew back as if scalded, standing tall and throwing back her hair.

Her face was red, her eyes dark green, and her fury enticing. She was absolutely stunning. "I am so going to kill you."

He couldn't help it. He burst out laughing.

Chapter Five

Ivy could barely stand. So many sensations and emotions blasted through her that she felt like she was on an upside-down roller coaster. Athan Maxwell had just spanked her. Their interactions had been nearly clinical and quickly performed for years. Sure, there had been moments of intimacy, some she'd held on to for eons with both curiosity and need. But this was different. Worse yet, although her butt smarted, her body felt alive...and needy—on fire. For him. Her breasts ached, and a determined pounding resonated from her clit.

She was furious and frighteningly aroused as she stood, her legs bracketed by his knees. Ones he'd easily flung her over. Given the look in his now cerulean-blue eyes, he was considering doing it again. She had to stand up to him, and now, or he'd never get the message. "If you ever think of doing that again, I'll have you arrested for battery."

His legs moved to press against hers, effectively capturing her in place. "Baby, you're in a rather precarious position to be threatening me. You might want to reconsider." His voice was a velvety smooth and dark rumble.

Her body reacted with heat at his tone, but her brain answered with intent. It was too late to back down. She wasn't the same terrified and dying farm girl who'd once had no choices regarding her existence. Now, she had not only choice but also power, and if he wasn't smart enough to realize that, she'd happily educate him. "Don't you ever call me *baby*. Not again." She threw strands of her thick hair away from her face. "That's an endearment for lovers. For males who can, you know, get it up." Yeah, she knew she was throwing a challenge in his face.

It was time she challenged him. Then she held her breath, wondering how he'd react. Part of her thought he'd cool off and disengage like he had so many times before. The other part, the one still tingling from his spanking, wondered...

He didn't let her curiosity last for long.

His hand snaked out faster than she would've ever imagined, grasping her neck and yanking her toward him. She had no choice but to grab his thighs to keep from going all the way down.

Then his mouth was on hers.

Her entire being quieted as if encircled by the eye of a hurricane. Then the world blew through her. Fast and hot, dangerous and deadly.

She fell into him, her eyelids fluttering shut, her nails digging into his pants. He kissed her, hard and wild, his tongue sweeping inside her mouth. She'd never felt anything like it. There were no feelings in the world like being kissed by Athan Maxwell.

She'd wondered for years, had dreamed for decades. With a soft moan, she kissed him back, accepting all he was finally giving her.

He stepped up into her, his mouth continuing to devastate any dream she'd ever had. One of his broad hands reached for her thigh and lifted her against him, easily moving her so her legs bracketed his waist. His other hand tangled in her hair, positioning her mouth beneath his as he took control.

All she could do was feel. Heat and danger, lust and fire. So much of it, and he poured every ounce down her throat to light her entire body aflame.

She ached.

She needed.

She craved.

They'd been tied together for longer than any human had ever lived, and she'd had no idea the heated depths churning within him. Not until right this moment.

Gasping for breath, panicking, she wrenched her mouth free.

He allowed it.

She gulped, panting to fill her deficient lungs. "Why?" she gasped, her body feeling foreign. Why now, after all this time?

"I've waited. This had to be your decision." His breath was hotter than any fire, nearly burning her forehead. "Just say the word, Ivy. I'll make you mine."

The words shocked her, while her body's instant reaction to him, one of hunger and aggression, stilled her. Warned her in a way she couldn't decipher. "I have to know the truth," she gasped, still unable to look above his whiskered chin. He had one of his hands intimately placed around her thigh, holding her against him. The other controlled her head by gripping her hair. Desire and something predatory, something terrifying, lay just beneath the surface of his powerful body. Did she have the courage to dig deeper?

"What truth?" His lips moved against her wounded temple, and she shivered.

The truth about her entire life. This mattered. She hadn't even known more was possible with him, and now, was it too late? Had he lied to her for decades? "Have I had freedom since we mated?" Her voice was low and breathy. Sexy. Like a siren of old on the silver screen and not like simple Ivy from an Irish village who no longer existed.

"You've been free," he said, his body solid rock beneath her hands. His chest was made of granite, and when she finally found the courage to look up, his eyes were the color of compacted slate. Deep and impossibly blue with golden shards.

Even though her body pounded with need, her brain fought for some rationale. "Have you been watching me?"

"Yes."

She blinked but didn't draw back. This felt too good. "For how long?"

His head cocked just slightly. "Since the beginning." A quick tightening at the corners of his eyes, rapidly gone, showed…surprise? At the question?

Since. The. Beginning. Thunder clapped through her, bringing a chilling freeze. "You've always watched me? Or had others do so?"

"Of course." The hand at her hip gripped tighter in a quick example of his strength. "You truly didn't think I mated you, put you in possible danger, and then just set you free, did you?"

Put like that, she sounded not only naïve but also downright stupid. She flashed back to the turn of the century when her loan application to build her first tenement house in the burgeoning city of New York had been approved. Then the time her stocks had suddenly doubled, or when her stockbroker had known exactly where to invest. "Have you controlled my entire life?" She withdrew her hands from his chest, leaving them empty and cold. How many decisions had actually been hers?

"Controlled? No." His hold didn't relent. "I may have steered you down a path or two, but you made your own decisions."

Yet she hadn't, had she? "Put me down." Before she started gyrating against him like a horny modern teenager.

He drew slightly away but didn't loosen his hold. "I need blood, Ivy." Without waiting for a response, he twisted his wrist and tilted her head to the side, revealing her neck.

"Be quick about it," she muttered, wishing her voice didn't sound so breathy. How had she thought him almost robotic? Unemotional? Raw stone with no depth? He wasn't. Not even close. He was churning fire and heated passion. Rough maleness and iron-clad control. There was so much to Athan Maxwell, and he was finally revealing himself. "Hurry up," she whispered. This was too much, and she needed distance to think and plan.

"Hmm." His lips skimmed her neck, and fire jolted to her core. "Maybe I've waited too long to make you mine. It's been absolute torture." Slowly, treacherously, he slid those twin fangs into her neck for the first time. He usually went for the wrist or upper arm, but this time, he took her neck.

Lust crashed through her to land between her legs. This was different and enticing in a way that made her head spin. Her body felt as if it belonged to somebody else, and the temptation to jump into the flames was overwhelming. *He* was overwhelming. He murmured something unintelligible, and his hand burned her flesh, even through the material of her dress.

His hold firmed, showing his strength and unreal power. In that second, she felt the immortal being at his core. This was beyond human and anything she could've ever imagined.

She gripped his flanks with her thighs, holding on with all her strength. She stiffened, every muscle tensing, and each nerve flaring wide awake inside her.

Swearing heatedly against her skin, his fangs deep and his mouth drinking rapidly, he yanked her dress up. Cool air brushed her thighs and smarting backside. Her breath caught, and her body angled closer to him. Wanting him. Craving something she'd only dreamed about alone at night.

What was happening? Was it possible to need this badly?

He slowly, treacherously, lifted the sides of her panties. Then he tugged, and the expensive silk shredded, removing the last barrier between them. The pads of his fingers were rough, and it was like he knew exactly how to tempt her as he tapped her thigh right where she ached so badly. For him. Just Athan—finally, something clicked deep inside her like a lock snapping shut. The feelings were too delicious to counter, and warning ticked through her, but it was too late. Her mind blanked, and her body took over. His first touch set her off, and she stiffened as an orgasm bore down on her, stealing her breath.

He murmured her name and moved that dangerous hand again, sliding first one and then two fingers inside her. The shocking invasion spurred her higher, and she clenched around him, wanting something just out of reach. He crisscrossed those talented fingers and brushed across a spot inside her she hadn't realized existed.

She arched against him, shutting her eyes and falling into the fire. Still drinking from her, he forced her to ride his fingers before pressing unerringly on her clit.

She cried out as a white-hot climax ripped through her with enough force to shove her head back into his hand. He moved his fingers, all of them, forcing her to ride out the waves until she collapsed against him, her forehead dropping to the muscles of his upper chest. His fangs retracted, and he licked the wound clean, making her shudder several times. Finally, she gathered the strength to pull away from his torso and look up at his dark gaze, her mind befuddled and her body zinging wildly.

"That's why I waited, Ivy," he murmured, the gold rimming the blue in his eyes again. "You give me an inch, and I'll own your body. It's the exchange. I need your blood, and I gain power over you in response. Make sure it's what you want, baby. Because if I get that power, I'll use it. I'll keep it forever."

Chapter Six

She shoved at him, so he slowly let her slide down his body and waited until she regained her balance before releasing her. The strands of her silky hair ran through his fingers, stoking the hunger gripping him even hotter. Finally being able to touch her barreled lust to his groin. His fangs started to descend again, and he focused solely on retracting them while shackling the beast at his core. He couldn't fully mate her until she understood all the repercussions.

But mate her he would.

He couldn't look away from her. How many times had he taken that green ribbon out of his pocket and run his fingers over it throughout time? The green had faded, and the sides had frayed, but the material was always with him. He'd reached for that tie more than once after a fight, finding comfort in his connection to her. But even then, he'd been careful not to mar the silk with blood, no matter how much of it he was losing.

God, she was gorgeous, her mouth swollen from his kiss and her face flushed from her orgasm.

"You son of a bitch." Striking out, she nailed him in the jaw with a right cross. Then she yelped, yanking her hand to her chest and cradling it, her eyes spitting fire.

"You know," he drawled, forcing his hands to remain at his sides and not on her hips where he wanted them. The immortal being deep down roared to take her to the ground and plant that marking on her ass for good, so he manacled his control with both hands. "I admit it's been a while since I've given a woman an orgasm—or two—but... I don't remember this being the response."

Her gaze dropped to his ankle, and her nostrils flared.

"I wouldn't," he advised, his breath heating. He'd been right and fair to give her more than a century to learn her strength and value, but he was finished with this defiance. His enemies were getting closer, and it was becoming impossible to stay away from her—not only on a strength level. Her brilliance and fortitude were a powerful draw and one he couldn't ignore any longer. "You've made your own way, lass."

"I haven't," she snapped, still holding her arm.

His nape itched. "Heal your hand and then we'll argue." He couldn't just stand there while she was in pain. "Did you break it?"

"No," she said, her lip slightly out in an adorable pout. "I may have cracked a couple of knuckles."

"Heal them." He didn't have time for stubbornness, and that pout made him want to cuddle her close. But if he touched her again, clothes were coming off.

She averted her gaze.

Instinct whispered down his spine. "You can't heal yourself, can you?" Damn it. Apparently, he wasn't the only one getting weaker by the year. It was time they mated. At the thought, the beast at his core roared, and blood pounded through his head, making his ears ring.

He'd grown to admire her through the years in addition to liking her, and his feelings for her had become more intense these last few decades. For ten years, he'd known this day was coming, but he'd also wanted to ensure that she had as much freedom as he could give her until it was too late. She faced him without backing away, and he had to admire even that. His mate truly was a brave little thing. "Come here, Ivy."

She swallowed but didn't move. Stubborn girl. Reaching out, he snagged her hair and gently drew her to him. "You're hurt. Stop being stubborn." Letting his fangs drop, he slashed open his wrist. "I could give you *my* jugular," he rumbled. The idea of her sweet mouth on his neck electrified his skin in a way he'd never felt before. The reality was nearly unimaginable.

Rolling her eyes, she reached for his hand and lifted it to her mouth, her skin unbearably soft against his. Taking a deep breath, she lowered her mouth and delicately drank his blood. Lightning flashed through him, and his cock strained against the zipper of his pants. Need and lust tightened his muscles, and he clamped down on desire. He'd never wanted anything or anyone more than he did Ivy O'Dwyer right now.

She finished drinking and pushed his hand away, licking her lips.

He groaned quietly, his hands nearly shaking with the need to touch her. But right now, they had to get a few things straight.

She looked toward the door. "I really do need to get on with my new life."

He smiled and was gratified when she took a step back. It was impressive how well she could read him after all this time. "We're both getting weaker, and you're obviously independent enough to make your own decisions now. We need to mate, Ivy."

She gulped. "We are mated."

Cute. She was playing dumb while scrambling for control. He got that. "Sex, bite, mark," he murmured, appreciating the damask-colored blush that slammed across her delicate cheekbones. "We have to meet four times a year now, and it's not enough for me." He lifted his chin, focusing on her now healed hand. "You can't heal yourself on your own. Both of us are going to become weaker, and we can't let that happen."

She inhaled and then slowly exhaled as if trying to calm herself. "I have to admit, I would like to try sex."

His cock pulsed in complete agreement.

She frowned, narrowing her gaze. "But then we go back to normal? Just meet up a few times a year for, well, sex?"

He bit back a laugh. His girl was cautious and pretty much adorable. "No. We plan a life together." With her safely away from his enemies. "We form a family and hopefully have sons." She was strong and smart, and she'd make an excellent mother. His boys would be lucky.

"Sons? There's a chance for daughters, right?"

"No. While demons can have females, vampires cannot. My people are much more vamp than demon, and we have boys." He wished it were different because he'd love to have a daughter. A mini-Ivy would be a delight to have around. "There's one exception, and it's unlikely to ever happen again."

She shuffled her feet in those fuck-me heels. "Well, I suppose we could give it a try." The rapid pulse rate he could hear inside her belied her casual tone. "You could come live with me as I finish this campaign to take predators off the internet."

Cute. "Actually, your time for courting danger is over. I'm happy to hire as many employees as you'd like to continue your work, but my calling hasn't changed." He figured she'd like the family holdings in Montana, and if she wanted to work from there, that was fine with him. But her role would be from behind a computer and not in the field. How had he missed her current profession?

"I don't think so," she said.

"You don't understand." He'd tried to explain reality to her before, but she'd never been ready to take the plunge. "There's an exchange, baby. I need your blood, and you need me." It was difficult to explain. "If you're taken away or killed, I die without your blood. If I stay alive, you need me near you for peace."

She rolled her eyes. "You're telling me I need sex from you? That I can't survive without your body?"

He snorted. "No. I've seen it happen once with a distant cousin, and the female mate went mad after what appeared to be crippling anxiety. I don't understand it, but the best we've figured out is that it's some type of pheromone-based need and reaction." It had been devastating to watch his cousin's mate implode after he'd been killed. Of course, that had been before the creation of the virus that could negate a mating bond. He explained such to her.

"As you know, I've heard of the virus," she said, waving a hand.

"I know. But understand that it has never been used with a mate who still had a living mate, and even if it works on you, I'd die." Most of the Realm doctors agreed that the virus wouldn't work on a mate unless their mate was long dead.

She tugged on a pearl earring as if deep in thought.

His phone buzzed, and he glanced down to see Jasper's number. He'd have to call him back. For now, he'd promised his older brother that he'd get answers. "You have some time to make a decision." Man, he hoped she didn't decide to let him die, but it had to be her decision. Every instinct he had whispered that she was too kindhearted to let that happen, but she'd still try to negotiate the terms. He liked that about her. A lot. For now, he had a job to do. "Ivy, where's Leah?"

Ivy's jaw firmed. "I have absolutely no idea."

As a liar, she was almost too cute for words, but she was definitely lying.

"How long have you and Leah been in touch?"

"I don't know what you're talking about," she said.

Impressive, that. "Where is she?"

"I honestly don't know," she said slowly as if speaking to somebody with a concussion. "Even if I did, I wouldn't tell you."

"I thought I just made it very clear to you not to defy me," he murmured.

Her tongue flicked out to wet her bottom lip. "Doesn't matter. I'm sure the second Leah saw you, she was long gone. Believe me, she has systems in place to make sure that even I don't know where she is."

That statement had a ring of truth to it.

"How long have you and Leah been meeting up?"

Ivy pressed her lips together as if refusing to let out any sound.

He couldn't believe it. He'd had her under surveillance for her entire life, yet he hadn't known she'd been meeting up with Leah. That spoke more to Leah's ability at subterfuge than Ivy's because he knew Ivy had not spent any time hiding. She'd been quite open about her whereabouts, and it rather surprised him that she hadn't realized he'd had a protection detail on her the entire time. Sometimes he forgot that even though she'd lived so long, she was still quite naïve.

"You need to tell me everything you know about Leah," he said, knowing Jasper would be calling again any second.

"No."

He just studied her. Raised voices came from the other room, along with a flurry of movement. He turned just as a knock sounded on the door. "Enter."

Klyde poked his head in. "You're not going to believe this. We just got word that Ulric is back on this world. The prison world failed, and he's alive and here somewhere."

Everything inside Athan chilled. Stone-cold, pure ice. "Are we sure?"

"We're sure. There was a fight outside of Butte, Montana the other day. He's back."

Athan settled into battle mode, plans forming in his head. "That means they're on the move, but it doesn't truly affect us. Who was in the fight?"

"It looks like the Realm, but they didn't kill him, and it *does* affect us. Rumor has it the leader of the Kurjans was killed."

Athan jerked, the battle plans instantly changing. "Dayne is dead?" Apparently, the time of their truce was over.

"Affirmative," Klyde said grimly. "That means Baston is off his leash."

Damn it. Sure, Athan knew the time would come, but he'd been hoping for another century or two before the Maxwell clan went back to war.

Klyde cleared his throat. "Since Ulric is back, the physics of this plane should return to normal. I mean, it should be harder and not so easy to morph shifters into werewolves, right?"

"Maybe," Athan muttered. "Who knows?" It'd be nice to stop hunting the weres all the time, especially since they now needed to hunt down Baston and his nephews if they wouldn't adhere to any treaty—which they wouldn't.

"Who's the Realm?" Ivy asked. "And who was Dayne and who is Baston?"

Klyde looked at her, nodded at Athan, and then shut the door as he left.

Well, this changed everything.

"The Realm is a coalition of immortal species including vampires, demons, and shifters. While we don't align with them, we are allies," he said, wishing he could protect her from this. Perhaps he should have told her all of this earlier, but he wanted her to at least have one or two good lifetimes before war came knocking on their door. "Dayne was the leader of the Kurjans, and Baston is one of his top soldiers. Kurjans are the worst species on the planet—I think they live for war."

She paled. "I've never met a Kurjan."

"You'd know it if you had," he said. "They're taller than us with black hair tipped with red, purple or red eyes, and very pale skin. The sun used to kill them, but their scientists have worked hard to change that." Yeah, he definitely should have explained all this to her earlier, but he'd wanted to protect her for as long as he could. "You have to know that this changes everything." He wanted to be gentle with her, but she had to realize that life was different now.

She grimaced. "Why?"

"Because Dayne is dead, and any treaty we had with him is now void. We had an agreement that while he was alive, Baston's family and the Maxwells would stay out of each other's way, mostly because we didn't want to deal in a war, and Dayne had his hands full with handling problems with the Realm. Baston doesn't care about the Realm and no doubt already has battle plans in place. Hunting season on the Maxwells has begun, and I'll have to take him out now." He probably should've done it earlier, but Grams had insisted they adhere to the treaty.

"Why? Why does this Baston want you dead?" she murmured.

"Same story as most wars—it's about a woman. My grams, to be exact." When she chose Athan's grandfather over Baston, war and death had ensued. Athan stared at his woman. He had to keep her safe. "I hate to do it, sweetheart, but I'm going to have to lock you down."

Chapter Seven

Ivy couldn't believe it. She one hundred percent and with the fury of a thousand suns could not believe that she was sitting in the back of a limo being forced to go to the airport—a private airport, no doubt. When Athan had said he was locking her down, he hadn't meant in Los Angeles. Apparently, she was about to fly to his family's safehold, wherever that might be.

Not that it mattered because she had most certainly not agreed to go dark.

Two vampire soldiers took positions in the front seat while she sat in the back, sipping a bottle of water. Athan had said he had business to take care of and would meet her at his holdings within the day, and even then, he wouldn't say where she was going.

Nor would he share details about his business, but surely it had something to do with the killing of this mysterious Dayne of the Kurjans. The second Athan had heard the news, something had changed in him. She'd seen it—perhaps felt it.

But he was different. Although his calm strength would probably always be present, there was a razor-sharp intensity that all but cascaded off him now. Apparently, hunting werewolves for him hadn't required this much stress.

He hadn't stopped to listen to what she wanted...or needed for even a second.

So now she sat in the back of a limo, trying to figure a way out. She had a job to do, and she was running out of time.

He hadn't even given her time to explain what she was going to do and what her new job was, as it seemed he hadn't figured that out yet.

Score one for Leah. When she created a super-secret organization, she did it right. Ivy had been smart to go into business with her at this time. Now, she just had to figure out a way to get there before their mark disappeared. They'd been hunting this guy for too long to let him get away now.

The driver turned down a private road that probably led to an airport used only by people in Athan's world. She stared at the forest blanketing the sides behind tall metal fencing with barbed wire at the top. No doubt there were cameras everywhere. She could run once they reached the airplane hangar, but it was doubtful she'd get far.

A motorcycle roared somewhere in the distance, and she perked up, her heart hammering. Was it the same attackers as before? The soldier in the passenger seat turned and craned his neck to see through the back window.

"What the?" he muttered.

Suddenly, projectiles crashed through all three windows in front. Smoke instantly began filling the vehicle.

"Damn it," the driver roared, slamming on the brakes.

Ivy lurched forward and dropped the water, extending one arm to keep herself from smashing into the back of the seat. She dropped to the wide floor, panic engulfing her. Pain ticked from her knees, and she shoved it away, bunching her body to move. The car slid into a skid and spun around.

Was it the same attackers as yesterday? She blinked to see, but the smoke was too thick. It burned her eyes and up her nose. She had to get out.

Coughing and holding her hand over her mouth, she scrambled to release the door and fell out and onto the asphalt. Dark pebbles cut into her knees. The attackers ran from the forest on both sides, standing on the opposite side of the fence. They were covered head to toe in black, and she couldn't make out their faces. She blinked and coughed, trying to see through the smoke. They lifted weapons and fired wildly at the vehicle.

The motorcycle spun to a stop, and a feminine hand reached down. "Ivy, let's go."

"Leah?" she asked, coughing again, panic nearly consuming her.

"Let's go," Leah said, grabbing her wrist and pulling.

"Stop," the driver yelled, falling out of the car, his large body denting the asphalt.

Ivy burst up and jumped onto the back of the motorcycle, wrapping her arms around Leah's waist. "Go, go, go," she yelled.

Leah laughed loudly and twisted the throttle, zooming away from the still-smoking vehicle.

Ivy coughed several times. "What was that?" she yelled.

"Just a smoke bomb. Nothing serious," Leah called back, the wind whipping her hair into Ivy's face.

Ivy turned her head, trying to see the forest on either side. "Who threw the smoke bombs?"

"A couple of guys I hired," Leah yelled back. "Hold on, we're going to have to go fast. I'm sure they're calling this in."

Oh, man, Athan would be pissed. Ivy bit back a chuckle. Something triumphant soared through her, and it was probably something she shouldn't be proud of. But he was always in control and telling her what to do—though it looked like she and Leah had just outsmarted him. She held on and ducked her head against the chilly wind as Leah drove like a maniac down the private road and then turned, zooming through the streets of LA.

There was no doubt CCTV caught them in several places, but Leah seemed to have a sixth sense for where to go. Or rather, she'd probably memorized the entire city and knew how to avoid the cameras. Finally, she drove them into an underground parking area and stopped at the far end. "All right, we have to switch vehicles now."

She waited until Ivy pushed off the motorcycle before following and shaking out her long, dark hair. She threw back her head and laughed.

Ivy brushed pebbles off her jeans. "How did you know where to find me?"

"Oh, please. Like I don't know where the Maxwells have their airports. Come on." Leah motioned toward a nondescript blue Chevy. "We have to go. We have a private flight waiting."

Ivy grinned. "You have this all figured out, don't you?"

Leah shrugged. "I figured we could have a problem some time or other, so I had a plan in place. Right now, we really have to get moving." She looked at her watch. "We're supposed to meet a possible kidnapper in about two hours."

Ivy sobered up. "You're right. Are you ready for this?"

Leah nodded. "Yeah, it's time."

* * * *

Athan sat very still in front of the video monitor as he watched his mate tool off on the back of a motorcycle. She looked fragile and in peril as they sped away with smoke in their wake. Enemies could be coming from any direction, and she was speeding away from certain safety. Oh, he'd definitely made a mistake in wanting her to enjoy freedom and her own destiny for a short time. Now, he had to find her. "Are you getting this?"

"Yeah, I'm getting it." Jasper was in Montana but showed in a box in the upper right corner of the screen, his irritation coming off him in visible waves. Athan would take a moment to appreciate that fact later—it was impressive. For now, it was clear his fury matched Athan's.

Athan shook his head. "This entire situation was well planned out."

"I'm aware," Jasper muttered. His hair was jet-black and his eyes an odd comingling of blue and green that was too electric to pass for human hazel eyes. Like some immortals, he normally wore colored contacts or dark glasses when in public. "Apparently, Leah has gotten even better at subterfuge than she was eighty years ago."

That happened when one mated a spy. But fate had her own plans, and Jasper's relationship was his to handle. However, there was nothing wrong with a little brotherly advice, especially since Athan's fucking mate was now in peril. He sucked in air, trying to ignore the fury pounding through his veins. "I think it's time you took your mate in hand."

"I plan to," Jasper muttered. "As soon as I find her."

Athan shook his head. "She's become quite good at evading you through the years. Hasn't she?" Although he couldn't really criticize right now, considering Ivy was out of his reach and sight.

"Yeah, she has, and I've allowed it to go on long enough."

Athan wondered where he should have drawn the line with Ivy. "I figured we had a little more time before Ulric returned home, and I really believed Dayne would live for centuries to come. I guess that was a mistake."

Jasper sighed heavily. "Agreed. I wanted to give Leah some freedom, too, but it's too late for that now. Our method of sending blood to each other is now in the past. I've given her enough time to get over her mad and make the right decision, but apparently, she's too damn stubborn. Do you have any idea where they've gone?"

"No. We're checking all the CCTV footage for the areas along the fence line and through town. But like I said, Leah seemed to have had this pretty well planned out."

Jasper's growl was low and barely discernible. "Okay, let's go at this from another angle. Do you know where Ivy's new life was going to be?"

"No," Athan said, scratching his head. He'd figured to discuss the matter with her after the funeral, but everything had quickly gone south. He'd never had a problem finding her before, although she seemed to be working with Leah now. "We're going through all data from here. I'm guessing she and Leah are working together and somehow set it up under the radar."

He truly hadn't been paying close enough attention. He'd been doing his best to stay away from her and let her enjoy freedom while she still had it. In doing so, he'd become complacent. She'd always been so sweet and kind, and she'd met up anytime he'd asked, so he had never pushed. She hadn't given him a reason to, and that was on him. He should have been paying closer attention. "There are a lot of things to be angry about from looking at this video," he murmured to his brother.

"No shit," Jasper returned.

Athan rubbed the back of his neck where a headache was forming. "Yet you know what's really bugging me?"

"What?" Jasper muttered.

"They're not wearing helmets."

Jasper barked out a laugh. "Your mate and mine just took off on a motorcycle clearly defying everything we've ever taught them, and you're worried about their heads?"

"Well, yeah," Athan said. "I know they're immortal, but everybody should wear a helmet. What if something happens?"

"Oh, something's going to happen," Jasper promised. "As soon as I find Leah, a lot's going to happen."

Athan nodded. "Agreed, but for now, we have to figure out where they went."

"They have to be staying in LA."

Instinct whispered otherwise. "I doubt it. Anytime Ivy has faked her death, she's moved to a different city." It was actually impossible to know where Leah had gone, but he didn't want to make Jasper any angrier than he already was. They needed to think clearly.

Jasper cleared his throat. "I'm sorry about this, brother."

Athan blinked. "Sorry about what? This isn't your fault."

"It is. I should have taken Leah in hand years ago."

"No," Athan said. "What's between you and your mate is between the two of you only. This is between Ivy and me. She knew better."

"I'll be in touch." Jasper ended the video call.

"Sounds good," Athan muttered to nobody in particular. He looked up at his soldiers around the room, all of them working furiously at consoles. "Has anybody caught sight of them?"

None of his men spoke. Damn it.

"Wait," Klyde said, leaning closer to his monitor. He frowned. "Um, I found something...odd." He swiped his hand and sent files to the main screen. "You're really not going to like it."

Athan wasn't liking *anything* right now. Still, it was a shock when several pictures of Ivy filled the screen. In the first, she was wearing a blond wig in pigtails and ridiculous black makeup. Her lips were cherry-red, and her eyes sparkling. Her body filled out the pink bra and panty set she wore nicely.

His chest heated, and his spine elongated. The next picture was of her pert backside in the pink panties, with his marking clearly visible in the center of her waist. Oh, it had faded through the years, but he could still clearly make out the M for Maxwell with the sharp and jagged lines around it. When an immortal with demon lineage found his or her mate, the branding mark of the first letter of their surname appeared on their palm to be transferred during the mating process.

His was perfectly formed in the center of her lower back for anybody to see.

He was too shocked to be angry. Nope. Fury hit a second later, and he stood, his body naturally bunching for a fight. He had to find her and now.

Chapter Eight

Exactly four hours after speeding away from a smoke-bombed-out vehicle, Ivy sat in a cheap motel room in Buffalo, wearing a long, blond wig with her face heavily made up with black eyeliner and purple lipstick. The torn black tank top covering her looked perfect with the ripped jeans. She sat in front of a brand-new laptop and chewed her gum nervously.

Leah checked her weapon. "Are you sure you're okay? I know you and Athan have had a congenial relationship through the years. That just changed, you know?"

Oh, she knew. "I'm ready for a change." It was time. While she had no idea what that change would be, she was finished living in a long-distance relationship. Either they'd try to make it together, or they'd go their own ways. "Is it all really true? Can they not live without our blood?"

"It's true," Leah affirmed.

Ivy typed rapidly on the keyboard in front of her, trying to find the private chat room. "Athan said that if we fully mated, I'd need him, too." He'd never told her that before probably because they hadn't intended to mate for a long time. "But you don't need Jasper."

Leah flushed from across the room. "I would if we were in the same vicinity. We only had sex that one time when we mated, and I started to crave him right away. It's part of the reason I ran." She pushed her dark hair away from her face. "The mating was a surprise for us both, and he needs my blood. I need him, but the craving subsides if I stay away long enough."

"Don't you get lonely?" Ivy murmured.

"Yeah," Leah whispered. She looked tough in her black jeans and shirt with her hair in a ponytail, and she had several inches of height on

Ivy. But vulnerability shone in her eyes. "I have to be in control of myself and my life."

"Or you have to trust your mate," Ivy said, staring at the monitor. The chat room was empty. She typed some more, trying to reach their current target. Getting him brought them one step closer to the mastermind behind what was a surprisingly organized group of assholes who tried to lure kids on the internet. "You and I have always been honest with each other, and I think the game you're playing with Jasper is somewhat enjoyable and challenging for you."

Leah tucked her gun into the back of her waistband. "You're not wrong."

"Someday, he's going to catch you." Ivy looked up at her friend.

Leah's dark eyes sparkled. "Maybe. We'll see just how good he is, right? I assume I'm even more on his radar now."

"I guess."

"How about some honest reflection yourself?" Leah stretched her neck as if preparing for a fight. "You've been in love with Athan Maxwell since the day he saved your life."

Well. That might be true, but it wasn't nice to say it. "Maybe. He's always been kind and funny when we've met up, and he kisses like a god. But that doesn't mean he loves me back."

"Have you given him the chance?"

Not really. But right now, she had a job to do. She'd figure out what she wanted to do with these new changes in Athan's life later. Regardless, she would like to engage in sex with him. She wanted him to be her first.

"Anything?" Leah asked, nodding at the laptop.

"Not yet." Frustration rolled through Ivy. She typed furiously on the keyboard.

Leah stood on the other side of the table, out of sight, her gaze worried.

Finally, a face came up on the screen. Ivy batted her eyes as if she were fourteen and clueless again. So, he had decided to make a move. It was about time. This guy was a pervert who had no problem trying to manipulate young girls, but like most creeps, he was a coward. Still, she'd seen the gleam in his eyes. He was ready to make a move that could hurt a child, and Ivy couldn't let that happen. "Harry. Hi. I wondered if you'd forgotten about me." She raised her voice several octaves to sound younger.

Harry Johnson smiled and smoothed his greasy hair back from his broad forehead. He was fifty years old, and the fake dye he put in his hair did nothing to hide that fact. "Hi there, Taylor," he said. "I thought you forgot about *me*." His voice held a thread of excitement that made her want to puke. "Thanks for the pictures you sent." His smile was too wide.

"Well, you said you wanted them." She hoped that Leah had been correct, and that the pictures would disappear within an hour. They'd been partial nudes, and she hadn't been happy about it, but she'd do what was necessary to catch this guy. Finally, she was doing something with the knowledge she'd gleaned over the last several decades. "So, we going to meet?" She twirled her hair around a finger.

Harry sat back and rubbed the stubble around his chin. Oh, he tried to dye it a darker color like his hair, but the white strands showed through. Apparently, he didn't know what he was doing.

"How about next week?" His eyes gleamed.

Her stomach slowly sank. "Well, yeah, but I'm at the motel now." She sounded every bit as confused as she felt.

He shrugged. "Yeah, I know, but I wasn't sure you were really going to meet me, so I made backup plans."

Behind the computer, Leah's eyes flared, panic crossing her face.

Ivy kept her voice calm and pouted. "You made other plans without me?" She tried to sound hurt, but her heart raced wildly.

They'd been trying to get this guy for nearly three months, and they'd thought they finally had him. It was no fun pretending to be an underage girl on the internet. But she and Leah had already taken out two of these bastards. "Harry?" She made her voice tremble.

"Like I said, you didn't seem a hundred percent sure, so I made alternate plans." He leaned toward the camera, excitement darkening his face. "I'm meeting somebody else tonight, but I promise I'll see you next time."

"No, wait." She held up both hands. "Are you in town?"

They'd come to Buffalo just for this so they could bring him down. He had to be close.

"Yeah. I am. I'll make arrangements to see you tomorrow night. Okay? We'll meet at the same hotel." He winked at her, blew her a kiss, and cut the feed.

Shock ricocheted through her.

"Damn it." Leah rushed for a computer on the other side of the room and started typing rapidly. "Oh, there he is. We've got him."

* * * *

"Are you ready for this?" Leah asked, slamming the clip into place in her gun.

"I think so," Ivy muttered, doing the same. She stretched her neck and tried to go loose. She'd never shot anybody before, but that didn't mean she wasn't ready to try. In fact, she had been going to a shooting range for the last decade or so. "Last resort is to kill this guy, right?"

"Right," Leah said grimly. "If he cooperates, we'll just turn him into the human police, like we did the last two we found. If not..." She let the threat trail off.

Ivy had absolutely no question in her mind that Leah would shoot if necessary. She had a small doubt whether or not *she* would, but hopefully she wouldn't have to find out. She was acutely aware that humans could die and she couldn't, which made this seem rather unfair. However, the guy was a predator who hunted young girls on the internet, so if anybody deserved to be shot, it was him.

"I can't believe you found him," she whispered to Leah as they both edged closer to the cheap motel, their gazes on the cracked purple door for room twelve.

"Once he clicked off with you, he was easier to trace than I thought," Leah admitted. "He's not as good as BlueEyes237."

Ivy frowned at just the name. They'd been hunting that guy since the beginning, and so far, he'd eluded them. He was as good at computers as Leah was, and that was saying something.

The only good news they had was that he seemed to be setting up the long game and had been connecting with Ivy over the internet for the past seven months. He didn't seem to be hunting any other girls. So as long as they kept his attention before finally finding him, she'd play the long game, as well.

She couldn't offer to meet because he'd be suspicious. Every one of these creeps made the move to meet. So, BlueEyes237 would probably be the same way, and they didn't want to scare him off. For now, they had to get inside this motel room.

As they got closer to the door, they could hear the drone of a TV and voices.

Ivy leaned forward and pressed her ear to the flimsy wood.

"You're older than I thought," a female voice said.

"Yeah, maybe. I'm sorry. I should've been more honest." It was

Harry's voice. Ivy knew it well.

A chill skidded down her back, and she tightened her hold on the weapon. *"They're in there,"* she mouthed to Leah.

Leah nodded. "I'll go around back. When you hear glass shatter, go in," she whispered.

Ivy nodded, her fingers trembling, and her stomach aching. Then she waited as Leah silently crossed around to the other side of the building and out of view. She continued listening in case she needed to go in before Leah was ready.

"I'm not sure I should drink this," the girl was saying.

"Oh, it's just a little bit of wine. You'll like it. It'll warm you up. Honest, all we have to do is talk, but let's at least have a drink together like old friends," Harry cajoled.

Oh, man. Ivy couldn't wait to have this guy arrested.

Glass shattered in the distance.

"What was that?" Harry roared.

Pivoting, Ivy leaned back and kicked the door by the doorknob like she'd been taught. The cheap plywood slammed open, hit the wall, and careened back at her. Grunting, she kicked it again and then moved in, her gun aimed at Harry.

Leah came rolling in from the bathroom, several cuts down her arm.

"What's going on?" Harry yelled.

"Sit down and shut up," Leah said, kicking him squarely in the back of the knee. He went down on his other knee and quickly jumped up, tackling Ivy into the wall. Pain detonated in her cheekbone while the torn wallpaper scratched her face.

She punched him hard in the nose, and blood spurted.

Leah kicked him in the back of the neck, and he went down on both knees. She pointed her gun at him, and he froze.

The motel room was cheap, with one bed and a dresser across from an old table with a box TV. A young girl sat on the bed, wearing jeans and a tank top, a glass of something red in her hand. She looked to be about twelve. Her eyes were blue, and she had her hair up in pigtails. She instantly started to cry.

"It's okay," Ivy said, moving for her. "You're all right."

"What are you doing here?" Harry boomed, starting to stand up.

Leah turned and executed a perfect kick to his face. He flew back, his head thunking against the table holding the TV. "Getting your ass arrested is what we're doing." She looked at Ivy. "Call 911."

"No," the girl said, holding up a hand. "Please, don't. My mom will kill me."

Ivy reached forward and slipped an arm around her shoulder, keeping her gun loose in the other hand. "I'm sure your mom won't kill you. Are you in danger at home?" She had to find out the whole truth.

The girl shuddered. "No, not really. I just... I don't know. We moved here, and I miss all my friends. And then I made friends with Harry. Except I thought he was only twenty and in college and..." The girl shook her head and started to sip the drink.

"Whoa," Ivy said, taking the cup away from her and sniffing it. The liquid smelled like wine, but she knew better. "What's in here, Harry?"

Harry blinked and frowned, squinting at her. "I know your voice."

"Yeah, you do. I'm TaylorTots," she muttered.

He looked her up and down. "You're older than you said."

"So are you," she retorted and then leaned toward the girl. "What's your name?"

"Susie," the girl said, looking at the smashed doorway.

"All right, Susie. Do you have any idea what was going to happen here tonight?" Ivy kept her voice gentle.

Susie paled and looked down. "I think I'm getting the idea. Honestly, I thought he was in college. He sent a different picture of a cute guy and said he was looking for models for a school project and I don't know. I was stupid."

"You weren't stupid. You're young," Leah said, reaching for zip ties from her back pocket. "You're going to need to tell the truth, though, okay?"

The girl gulped and nodded. Movement sounded by the door, and Athan suddenly filled the space, so much energy rolling from him that the already frightening aura of the room swelled and heated to something even more dangerous.

Chapter Nine

Athan took in the scene with a glance and then all of it made sense. He looked at Ivy. "The pictures of you on the internet? You're operating some sort of trap for pedophiles?"

She grimaced and stood between him and the shaking girl on the cheap bedspread. "Yeah, it's my new job, and I'm not done with it, so I'm not going anywhere until we finish the cases we have."

"Cases?" he muttered. What in the hell was going on here? "You're not a cop, Ivy." He looked at Leah. "And you're not going anywhere."

Leah showed no fear but started edging toward the bathroom at the back of the room.

Athan growled. "I'm not kidding."

Klyde then emerged from the bathroom with no cuts showing on him. He must have avoided the glass on the window, unlike Leah, if the dots of blood down her neck and arm were any indication. Klyde looked around. "What have we walked into?"

Athan looked at the asshole blubbering on the floor. "I have a feeling we have a guy who's going to jail." He craned his neck to see beyond Ivy. "We also have a witness"—his gaze encompassed Ivy and Leah—"and a couple of wayward mates who are about to move to headquarters."

"Fair enough," Klyde said, eyeing his watch. He'd been Athan's right hand for centuries, and once he'd discovered computers, he'd fallen in love. Klyde disliked being away from his laptop for long, but he was excellent in the field. Plus, he was Athan's best friend as well as his brother.

Leah rapidly zip-tied Harry while Ivy reached for the phone on the bedside table and dialed 911. She handed it to the girl. "Call it in and tell them everything."

The girl, her voice shaking, quickly gave a rundown of the entire situation, and the 911 dispatcher said help would be there in a minute. Her voice was loud, and she sounded competent. The girl ended the call, set the phone back in the cradle, and scooted farther up on the bed, putting her back to the wall and pulling her knees to her chest. While she still looked scared, anger had started to infuse her young face with color.

"All right, let's go," Athan said, slinging an arm around Ivy as Klyde gently gestured Leah toward the door. "We don't need to be here when the human police show up. He is secured, and you're okay, right?" he asked the girl.

The girl nodded and stared at Harry on the floor. Sirens could be heard in the distance. She reached for the phone on the table. "I'd better call my mom."

Ivy stiffened. "Have you talked to any other boys on the internet like Harry?"

"No," Susie said. "Just Harry, who I thought was a hot college guy." She glared at him. "You're a perv, dickhead. And if you think I won't happily testify against you, you're wrong." She dialed the phone and lifted the receiver to her ear. "Mom?"

"Move," Athan said. "We need to be gone." They needed to avoid human officials since they never died, and they had to avoid the news media at all times. He hustled Ivy out the door with Klyde and Leah behind them. Lightning cracked high above. They hurried across the parking lot to a dark SUV waiting silently near a darkened forest. Thunder rolled, and rain started to pelt down.

"Get in," Athan said, opening the back door and blinking away the punishing rain.

Panic crossed Ivy's face, and she looked at Leah. In one smooth move, Ivy pulled her gun from her waist and pointed it at him, backing away. "Sorry, but I'm not going with you."

Leah edged away from Klyde, her gun also out. Klyde looked more bemused than angry as he reached out, knocking the weapon from her hands.

Athan held on to his patience. Apparently, they needed to set some parameters. The idea that his mate would point a weapon at him was a little much right now, considering he'd had to chase her across the country only to find her in a possibly dangerous situation. Oh, the jerk in the hotel room was human, but that didn't mean he couldn't hurt her.

Neither she nor Leah was trained to deal with criminals, and the thought that they were doing so caused irritation that was getting more difficult to ignore—although he admired their intentions. "Give me the gun." He held out a hand.

Ivy hesitated, her hold lightly trembling on the weapon. Then, smooth as silk, she turned and fired rapidly at Klyde, hitting him several times in the chest. Klyde flew back against the vehicle, denting the door. "Run, Leah," Ivy yelled. "Run now."

Leah paused for a second and then turned and sprinted into the forest.

Shock trilling through him, Athan grabbed for Ivy's gun. She turned, effectively kicking him in the knee and then performing a high kick to his jaw. His head snapped back. Then she fired several times into his upper thigh.

Pain exploded in his leg. Growling, he snatched the gun out of her hand and grabbed her by the neck, putting her against the vehicle with enough force to jar but not hurt her. Grunting, he mentally shoved the bullets out as Klyde stirred on the ground, rain drenching his hair and mingling with the blood pouring from beneath his white T-shirt. "Klyde?" he muttered.

Klyde groaned and sat up. A bullet popped out of his chest. "What the hell?"

Athan looked toward the now silent forested area and then down at his damaged thigh. Blood soaked his jeans and ran down to his knee. "Can you run?"

"No," Klyde muttered, grasping his chest. "I have three more bullets to push out. What the hell is up with my brothers and their mates?"

Athan concentrated and popped another bullet out of his leg. There was no way they were going to catch Leah. Surprise and anger percolated in his bloodstream, along with the necessary healing cells. He looked down at his mate, who was also staring at the forest, her expression way too calm considering she'd just shot him.

He tightened his hold on her. The brat wasn't going anywhere.

* * * *

Ivy's hands had been chilled since she'd shot Athan and Klyde.

She'd actually *shot* them.

Sure, they were immortal and already healing themselves, but she'd never shot anybody before. The coppery smell of blood filled the SUV the entire way through the city with Athan driving and Klyde in the passenger seat. Every once in a while, Athan would grunt, and Klyde would groan as they no doubt expelled the bullets from their bodies.

Ivy sat in the back seat, buckled in, the doors secured with child locks. She couldn't get out, and it was a little irritating. Her face still ached from Harry slamming her into the wall, and she tried to send healing cells to her cheekbone, but nothing happened. A long time ago, after she and Athan first mated, she'd been able to somewhat heal herself from injuries. That ability had disappeared about thirty years ago. She missed it.

Another bullet fell out of Klyde's chest to ping on the floor.

She winced. While she'd fire again to help Leah escape, she did regret causing them pain. She cleared her throat. "How did you find us?"

Neither male answered.

She crossed her arms and watched lights go by outside. It wasn't like she could blame them for being irritated. Make that pissed off. While Klyde seemed more resigned to healing himself, Athan was angry. She knew that much because his anger swelled throughout the vehicle, and goose bumps rose along her arms. Her breath quickened, and she had to concentrate to lower her breathing and heart rate. Those meditation classes her last identity had attended came in handy very often.

Athan cut her a look in the rearview mirror, and her entire body froze.

Forget angry. He was furious.

They drove through the town of Buffalo and finally maneuvered into a private parking garage, passing through several automatic gates to do so. The garage lay underground, beneath what appeared to be about a ten-story building. The structure was brick and at the end of town, surrounded by townhouses and what looked to be high-end restaurants and stores.

It was dark and innocuous but looked solid. Protected.

Ivy's heart sank. She really needed to learn how to be a cat burglar during one of her lives.

Athan drew the vehicle to a stop at the far end of the parking garage, which already held several dark and sparkling SUVs with shaded windows. Each could be occupied, and she'd have no clue. He cut the engine and stepped out of the vehicle, swearing softly under his breath. No doubt his leg still hurt. With smooth and economical motions, he pulled open her door and held out a hand.

She paused, indecision holding her in place. Then she gingerly placed her hand in his, instantly feeling a jolt of heat rush up to her shoulder. A quick glance at his rugged face revealed absolutely nothing...except the fiery goldish slices through his normally calm eyes.

When she tried to draw back, he pulled her out.

Silently, they made their way to the elevator and rode quietly upward. Klyde exited on the eleventh floor, not looking back. The doors closed again, almost in slow motion. Ivy leaned against the wall, her heart feeling like the small organ had climbed right into her throat. Smoothly, the doors opened to reveal a penthouse apartment with sparkling white tile, gray leather sofas, high-end artwork, and a wide wall of windows that showed the city at night.

She walked out with her head held high and waited until Athan followed suit. "Is this your place?"

"No. I'm meeting a friend here tomorrow. He said we could use the top two floors." Athan leaned back against the doors and crossed his arms. He was a foot taller than her, at least, and there was no doubt he was stronger.

She sighed. "I know you're mad."

One of his dark eyebrows rose. "Mad?"

She gulped. Then her body took over, and she retreated several steps.

"There's nowhere to go, Ivy," he said softly. Too softly.

The hair stood up on the nape of her neck. He'd spanked her when she'd merely kicked him. What would he do to her now that she'd shot him? "I didn't have a choice."

"You always have a choice." He moved almost casually toward her.

She took another step back. "I had to help Leah escape."

"No, you really didn't." He reached her and ran his knuckles gently over her aching cheek. "You can't heal that?"

She swallowed and looked down at his bloody thigh. "No. How about you?"

"I ejected the bullets, but I'm having difficulty healing the wounds." He pushed her hair away from her face, sending spirals of awareness down her torso to land hard between her legs. For years, it had gotten more and more difficult to be near him and not react. Each time after giving him blood, she'd been in a constant state of need and curiosity for days. Slowly, he lowered his head, giving her plenty of time to move away.

She held her breath and didn't move.

Then he kissed her. Deep and hot, he dove in, his hand flattening across her lower back to pull her body flush against his. He was one long line of solid muscle and strength, and she moaned right into his mouth.

Pleasure slid through her, peaking her nipples and seizing her lungs. Her thighs softened. Heat blasted and fired her every nerve.

He leaned back, his hand a solid weight across her shirt. "It's time, Ivy."

It wasn't a momentous declaration of love, but the simple words still shot desire rippling along her skin. "You're mad at me."

"I'm pissed," he agreed, his gaze darkening. "We'll deal with you shooting me later, and you probably owe Klyde Raider tickets for the next decade. For now, the fact that you shot me shows you're not remotely afraid of me, which is what I've needed from you. If you decide to mate, you're doing so of your own volition. This is your decision."

They were already mated as far as she was concerned. But every ounce of her being wanted to complete the act. Then at least they could have sexual relations every time they met up to exchange blood. It was just a new facet of their relationship, and she wanted it. "We're not going to agree on many things," she warned him.

He glanced down at his bloody leg. "I'm well aware of that, mate."

She wanted this. They both needed the strength of being able to heal themselves, and the only way to do that was to finally take the plunge. Even without that factor, she'd say yes. It wasn't just curiosity...it was Athan. She'd seen beneath his solid core of calmness and control more and more over the years. Now, she wanted to dive right in. Completely. She definitely wanted *him*. All of him.

So, she jumped for him, wrapping her arms around his neck, clamping her legs around his waist, and smashing her mouth down on his.

Chapter Ten

Desire deepened in him as he caught her, holding her aloft. She'd jumped into his arms of her own volition. Wanting him. Offering herself. In that second, he wanted to devour her.

His feelings for her, his raw *need* for her, had been building decade by decade, and now she was finally pressed against him. It was important that she'd made the first move, and now he could take over. Take *her* the way he'd wanted for so long. He wanted to taste her sweet skin, and then he wanted to do it again until he owned every soft inch.

He let her direct the kiss for a few more seconds, enjoying the feeling of her silky lips against his. Then he took over, pressing her head back while holding her aloft. Lust poured through him on the heels of something deeper. A sensation he'd only ever felt for Ivy O'Dwyer. Protectiveness, possessiveness, and raw hunger. The feeling slaked him, clawing through his nerves and burrowing beneath his skin with a demand that was so close to finally being appeased.

God, he wanted her.

It had been nearly impossible the last decade to leave her each time he tasted her blood, but the wait had been worth it. She was in his arms, her mouth open beneath his by choice.

Her blood tasted like ripe honeysuckle, and her mouth was even sweeter. Like honeysuckle mixed with smooth vanilla. Murmuring, he released her mouth and kissed across her high cheekbones to nip her beneath the jaw, turning and walking toward the master bedroom of the place. He'd stayed here several times through the years and was familiar with the layout. Even so, he tuned in to the world around them, making sure there were no threats waiting inside or coming for them outside. The elevator locked automatically, and he didn't scent anybody else in the place, so he could relax and concentrate fully on Ivy.

Finally.

She tunneled her hands through his hair, her nails scraping his scalp with an erotic bite. He reached the bedroom and let her slide down his body, tucking his fingers beneath her skimpy tank top and pulling the soft material up at the same time. The backs of his knuckles brushed the swells of her breasts as he tugged it over her head and dropped the material carelessly on the plush carpet. Then he leaned back and indulged himself by looking his fill as she stood in front of him, so small and fragile but frantically trying to rip the buttons on his shirt free.

Her bra was pink with a front clasp. "How convenient," he murmured, snagging the hook open with one finger. The lace flipped wide, and he growled, lust landing hard in his groin. A cute smattering of freckles covered her creamy breasts with their light pink nipples. His girl was a true Irish rose with the coloring to boot. She'd burn to a crisp in any sunshine. "You're beautiful."

As he said the words, a lovely damask flush started in her spectacular chest, climbed up her neck, and filled her face. He watched, fascinated. "So lovely, Ivy." This was her first time, and he wanted it to be special for her. The moment she decided to give herself to him, it had become beyond special to him. But he had to be careful not to hurt her. "If I scare you, let me know."

She rolled those stunning green eyes. "I'm modern, Athan. I'm not scared of you."

Good. She shouldn't be frightened of him in this context. Not when they were together and intimate. He'd deal with her lack of concern for his temper and her newfound penchant for shooting him later. Right now, she needed to know that she was safe—and wanted.

If he wanted her any more, he'd fucking explode.

For the first time in his entire life, his hands trembled as he slid them down her chest to cup her breasts. As a male always in control, the idea shook him, but he couldn't stop now. Her honeysuckle scent wrapped around them both and slid down to prod the dangerous beast at his center. The second he touched her, those succulent nipples peaked, hardening to the texture of diamonds against his palms.

They both groaned.

He caressed her and added a bit of bite, noting her quickening breath. His mate liked a bit of pain as well as a show of dominance, which was a good fucking thing because he didn't know how to be any other way—not in the bedroom or anywhere else in his life. Her path would be an easy one outside the bedroom if she remembered that. If not, there would be lessons to be learned. But not here. Here, she was safe and responding as well as he could've ever dreamed. Paying close attention to her breathing, he gently tweaked both nipples.

She caught her breath and leaned into his hands, her heart pounding loud enough that he could hear it.

Perfect. She was absolutely fucking perfect. He tugged gently again, and she gasped, pleasure pouring from her. Even so, her eyes widened. She was overwhelmed and starting to appear a mite panicked from the multitude of sensations.

So, he planted one hand on her upper chest and pushed her onto the bed.

She bounced twice, gasped in surprise, and then burst out laughing. Good. She needed to know that this was fun, too. He smiled and let his hands go to his belt.

Her gaze followed his movements, and her eyes widened. She licked her bottom lip.

Yeah. She was everything he could ever want. Slowly, he withdrew the belt from the loops, noting her quickening of breath. Nice. Then he shoved down his bloody jeans, making sure to partially twist to the side so she couldn't see the bullet holes. He was fully erect and ready, and her eyes somehow widened even more, pure panic in them this time.

"You're all right," he murmured, setting one knee on the bed. Then he moved slowly, efficiently unbuttoning and then unzipping her torn jeans and tossing them easily over his shoulder to make her laugh. His gaze caught on the barely there triangle of material covering her sex, and he growled low, unable to help himself.

* * * *

That low growl licked across Ivy's skin. She could barely breathe but didn't much care. Athan Maxwell was in front of her, utterly nude, fully erect. He was one incredible and slightly intimidating male. Make that full-on intimidating. His chest was raw muscle, cut hard. His abs were strong and countable, and below those...his cock visibly throbbed.

Everything inside her softened with need. An edge of caution rode her hunger, and wetness coated her thighs. Her now *bare* thighs. She'd never cared much about her physical appearance since she changed it with every lifetime, but right now she did.

As if he could read her thoughts, he smiled and slid his hands up her flanks, causing fiery eruptions along the way. "You're stunning, Ivy. Every fucking inch of you," he whispered.

She'd never heard him swear. At his statement, which sounded like a vow, she actually felt beautiful. Wild and free and with him. "So are you," she said, meaning it as her voice trembled. How did he even exist? Sure, he was immortal, but even so, the hard-cut angles of his entire body were unreal. Not only could she see his obvious strength, she could also sense his power.

So much more than she'd realized.

As if sensing she was retreating into her mind, he leaned over and placed a kiss on her right hip bone. Trembles cascaded down her legs. Smiling, he nipped the other hip bone, shooting spirals of electricity right to her core. Then he moved, right there, and she sucked in a breath. "Wait, Athan, I—"

He kissed her there. Right on her clit. The sensation was wet and hot and fiery. She gasped, leaning up into his mouth. He settled in, his broad shoulders pushing her legs apart as he ever so gently kissed her again.

Tears sprang to her eyes, and then need crashed through her entire body, His chin settled at the base of her slit, and then his tongue and mouth started to drive her absolutely wild. She'd had no idea. Sure, she was aware of the mechanics of this, but the feelings? The actual raw, frantic, delicious feelings were a shock. All too soon, she was climbing. Hot and fast, desperate and wild...she broke, crying out his name.

She'd barely come down, murmuring, when he drove her up again. His fingers were everywhere, his mouth so hot it was as if he'd eaten fire. Her second orgasm had her screaming, and her third had her whispering. The fourth stole her breath and pretty much shut down her mind.

Then, and only then, did he climb up her body and settle his mouth on hers. He kissed her, tasting of honeysuckle, his lips firm, and his tongue demanding.

She returned his kiss, giving him everything she'd ever be. Her breath hitched as he slowly penetrated her, filling her too fast when he wasn't close to being all the way inside her. Several times he paused, his forehead lowered to hers, his hands and talented fingers working her breasts, hips, and buttocks. Sensations bombarded her from every direction, so she let herself just enjoy as she eagerly explored his body, filling her palms with muscle and strength.

Pain began to filter through the pleasure, and she stiffened.

Then he shoved all the way inside her, pushing past every barrier and taking her completely.

She cried out, arching against him, her eyes opening wide as she tried to push him away.

His wild, sapphire gaze met hers, his eyes filled with sharp gold shards. Pain echoed through her, and tears filled her eyes, spilling down her cheeks.

Looking invincible, appearing deadly, he gently leaned down and licked the tears from her cheeks. She shuddered. He kissed her then, taking her under, mimicking with his tongue what he was about to do with his body.

Then he started moving. Slowly at first, and then with more force.

The pain turned to a desperate pleasure. Or rather, the pain and pleasure melded together until she couldn't tell the difference and no longer cared. It was only sensation after sensation, feeling after feeling, hunger after need that filled her with Athan. He was in her, around her, taking her. He tucked one arm beneath her thigh and lifted it on the bed, allowing him to go even deeper.

He hit a spot inside her that had her crying out and digging her nails into his upper arms. More. God, she needed more. "Faster," she moaned.

He obliged, growling, one arm around her thigh and the other sliding beneath her waist to lift her to meet his powerful thrusts. There he paused, both arms securing her as his body controlled her, pressing her into the mattress. He leaned down and brushed his mouth against hers as tension and hunger filled the air around them. "Mine, Ivy. Tell me you get me." His tone was rough, and his voice guttural. Full-on, demon guttural as if he'd been swallowing both gravel and shards of glass.

She gulped.

The arm holding her thigh twisted, allowing his hand freedom to slide up and tweak her nipple. Hard. "Now."

She gasped, liquid heat slashing right to her core. "I got you. Yours," she moaned.

"Tell me you'll obey."

She jerked. "No."

"Yes." He kissed her hard, his mouth unrelenting. "I'll teach a lesson here if you want."

She didn't want a lesson. She wanted him. "Fine. I'll be as safe as I can be." The words tumbled out of her, and she needed him to move again.

Then he did. Hard and fast, he took her high, forcing her over the cliff in an orgasm so spectacular she saw stars. She moaned his name this time, too overcome to scream.

He pounded even harder and then dropped his mouth to her neck, sliding his fangs into her soft flesh and digging deep to the bone. The pain was unbearable, but she was still riding that orgasm, and the sensations all burst together into a feeling that was fire and ice combined. Heat flared along her upper back as his marking landed right where it had been placed before, and she felt that branding flow into her blood and course through her entire body. Another orgasm shattered her, and she shook wildly with the aftershocks.

Groaning against her neck, he shuddered with his release.

Gasping, trying to breathe, she slid her palms down his back and dug in.

He lifted his head, and his eyes had morphed to a raw and deep gold rimmed with blue. Incredible. "You made the vow, baby," he said, his voice hoarse. "I'm holding you to it."

She gulped, overcome by him. Every cell in her being felt like his. Full-on...*his*.

Chapter Eleven

Athan left Ivy sleeping peacefully in bed, his mind clear, and his body calm. Finally. Oh, they had a lot to figure out, but at least they were on the same page. He sensed Benjamin Reese in the living room before he detoured through the kitchen for a large cup of coffee and drank half of it down before seeing his old friend lounging in one of the gray chairs, typing rapidly on a smartphone. "I thought I locked the door."

"It's my penthouse," Benny said easily, still texting. Then he looked up, his luminous eyes mellow and his hair a mess to his shoulders. "I smell sex."

Athan sighed and took the adjoining chair. "Benjamin. That's my mate you're talking about."

Benny tossed the phone onto the sofa. "It's about damn time." He grinned. As an immortal, Benny was overlarge, and that wasn't counting his personality, which was a cross between massive and insane. Athan had always figured Benny used the odd personality as a front. "Where is she? I want to congratulate her." His voice was booming.

Athan shook his head. "She's sleeping. How's Karma?" Benny had mated Karma, adopted her two human girls, and then promptly impregnated her three times, having boys.

"She's great. About to get pregnant again, I'm sure." Benny sat back, overwhelming the plus-sized chair.

"That's amazing. Congrats," Athan murmured, taking another drink of the too-strong brew. It was difficult for immortals to procreate, and it often took centuries for siblings to be born.

Benny nodded. "Right? I mean, if you think about it, there's a reason the Kayrs family has ruled the Realm, and the Kyllwoods, the demon nations. They just have more kids than anybody else, so they have more security, and there's always somebody ready to step up. Never thought I'd follow that path."

Athan's eyebrow rose on its own. "You want to lead a nation?"

"Fuck, no." Benny tipped back his coffee mug. "But I wouldn't mind owning a continent or two, you know?"

Athan had no idea. "Sure."

"The Maxwells had a bunch of kids, right?" Benny's face was square and rugged, and his shoulders were too broad for his shirt. "It's really too bad about your curse. Or I guess it's all genetics these days. You probably have some weird mutation." He leaned forward, planting his elbows on his knees. He wore a new blue flannel shirt and dark jeans, no doubt insisted upon by Karma. "There might be a cure, you know."

"I'm well aware," Athan said. "One of my brothers has had contact with the queen. Hopefully, she'll find the answer." The queen of the Realm was a brilliant geneticist determined to figure out all the immortal species. Although did the Maxwell clan truly *want* an answer? For centuries, fate had helped them to find their mates, and their bonds were unique. The Maxwell curse very often turned out to be a blessing, and who would they be without that? He forced himself back to business and the Kurjans. "Dayne is dead?"

Benny nodded somberly. "Yeah. Paxton Phoenix killed him with Garrett Kayrs holding him still. The Kurjans have placed bounties on both their heads, but right now, we're more worried about Ulric's return."

Ulric was the psychotic leader of the religious arm of the Kurjans, but he wasn't Athan's problem right now. "I'm concerned about Baston. What do you know?"

"I know the treaty in place between the Maxwells and the Kurjans is now over since Dayne is buried deep," Benny said in a rare and somber moment. "He's coming for your grams."

"Intel?" Athan asked, his mind settling into strategy. Nobody threatened his family. Period.

"Not much." Benny grimaced. "We have an operative in Kurjan headquarters right now, and Baston's on the move. He has three nephews working exclusively with him, and they've scattered wide and far to find her. The bounty on your gramps, alive or dead, is the highest I've ever seen, and the one on your grams, alive only, is comparable. I hope they're locked down."

Athan grimaced. His grandparents most certainly were not locked down. "I'm sure Cathal is trying to put my grams in a safe place, but she's, um, stubborn." After a century or two, most immortals resorted to first names, even for parents and grandparents to avoid confusion if humans were around. It would be odd to call someone who looked mostly the same age by the name of *Gramps*. Yet Grams would always be Grams to Athan. "Do you have any other intel, Benny?"

Benny eyed the closed door to the master bedroom. "Just that trouble is coming, my old friend. A bunch of elements and situations I can't discuss are about to come to a head, and I'm not sure what will happen. I'm securing my family far away from the Tetons, just FYI."

As a warning and a hint, it was helpful. "We've fortified the Montana base." There was no reason to be coy with Benny, considering he'd visited the family holdings more than once throughout the years. "Are we going to be affected by whatever you're involved with now? Whatever the Seven might be?" He took pleasure from the surprise that flickered in Benny's deep eyes. "Yeah. We have resources, as well." The Seven were an immortal group somehow fighting Ulric, and Benny was one of them. An oddity to be sure.

"I don't know." Benny always gave the truth, which was one of the reasons Athan put up with his *uniqueness*. "If you're affected, then so is the entire world. We're doing our best, but the end is coming soon. Trust me."

Athan nodded. "I do. If you require my assistance, I expect a call."

"Always." Benny scratched his rock-solid jaw. "You're smart to finally finish this mating, or complete it, right now. Just in case the world blows up or something."

Athan sighed. "Care to tell me more?"

"Can't. You just worry about Baston and his nephews. He's, ah...he hasn't given up on your grams. With the new virus and all." Benny winced.

Irritation flared throughout Athan. "The female has been mated for three millennia."

"Some chicks are hard to forget," Benny drawled.

Athan sighed. "Don't call my grams a chick."

The elevator doors opened to reveal his grandparents. "I couldn't agree more," his grandfather boomed, escorting his mate out.

Athan immediately stood. "What in the world are you doing here?"

His grams smiled serenely. "Apparently, we're back to war." She clapped her hands authoritatively. "Let's finish it this time, shall we?"

* * * *

Ivy steeled her shoulders, patted her hair in place, and then walked out of the bedroom as if nothing had happened. As if she hadn't had wild sex all night and now felt Athan Maxwell in every cell of her entire being.

She stopped short at seeing him standing in the living room next to Benjamin Reese and two people she didn't know. She had met Benny a few times through the years, and he had always seemed like a gentle giant to her. Heat flushed through her face, and she fought the insane urge to run back into the bedroom. Instead, she walked toward Athan as if she had every right to do so—which, frankly, she did.

He snaked out an arm to pull her close, facing the newcomers. "Ivy, I'd like you to meet my grandparents. This is Nia and Cathal Maxwell."

Ivy blinked and tried to appear normal.

"Oh, it's so very nice to meet you." Nia rushed forward and clasped both of her hands around one of Ivy's. "I've been on Athan to bring you to the ranch for so long. I never thought it would happen."

Ivy gulped. If there was anything in the world Athan's grams did not look like, it was a grandmother. The woman was definitely the most beautiful person Ivy had ever seen in real life—or even as airbrushed. She stood about five feet, two inches and had deep brown eyes flecked with gold, a side smattering of freckles, and a wild mane of hair that right now was in beautiful coils down her back. Her bone structure was delicate, and her skin was a dark tawny touched by the sun. It was impossible to tell her heritage, but a very slight Scottish brogue danced in her tone. Of course, considering the woman was probably about three thousand years old, she may have only lived in Scotland for a time and picked up the accent.

"It's nice to meet you," Ivy said, curiosity flourishing in her as she looked at Athan's grandfather. There was no doubt they were related. Cathal was as tall as Athan with stunningly dark blue eyes, an unruly mass of lighter brown hair, and shoulders wider than Benny's. He looked like a slightly older version of Athan and wore dark jeans and a white button-down shirt.

"Hello," he said, reaching out and quickly shaking her hand. "It's about damn time Athan brought you into the fold."

Athan rolled his eyes. "Ivy and I have been on our own schedules, and you two know it. Now, back to business. Why are you here?"

Cathal rolled his neck. "You're off werewolf and Kurjan scientist duty. I just sent Klyde to take over that part of the family business." He shifted a weapon to a better position strapped to his massive right thigh. "I smelled bullets on him, but he'd already healed himself. Who shot him?"

Athan lowered his chin but didn't answer.

Ivy cleared her throat. "Um, I did."

Cathal flicked his blue gaze her way. "Interesting."

Nia chuckled. "Can't wait to hear that story."

Cathal looked at Benny and then at Athan. "Ben, you staying for a while?"

"No," Benny said, glancing at his watch. "I need to get back. It's unlikely that Karma's pregnant again quite so soon."

Athan snorted. "You know it's a joke, but you're going to end up with a dozen just like you, Ben."

Benny paled. Then he winked at Ivy. "It's good seeing you, girl. We'll spend more time together soon. I'll have Karma and the kids with me, and we'll have a grand time." He jerked his head toward the elevator. "Athan? Before I go, I have an informant on ice waiting to speak with you."

Athan stiffened. "Why didn't you just say so?"

"I was doing the niceties," Benny said, frowning. "It's what friends do." He loped toward the elevator.

"I'll come with you," Cathal said, following him. "I take it the guy on ice pertains to my business?"

"Yep," Benny said.

Within a few seconds, the men were gone.

Nia looked at Ivy and then grinned. "They're such dorks. They may live thousands upon thousands of years, honey, but let me tell you, they remain idiots." Her tone was soft, her smile sweet, and her eyes sparkled in a way that had Ivy laughing and instantly relaxing.

"Well, that's good to know," she said. "It really is."

Nia put an arm around Ivy and pulled her close, even though she was several inches shorter. She wore a light blue sundress with sparkling gold heels. "Now, come tell me what you've been up to because rumor has it that you and Leah have been in touch. I would love to hear how that girl is doing. I sure miss seeing her."

Ivy stumbled and then let Nia lead her toward the living room. What could she say? She didn't want to give Leah away, but Nia seemed to genuinely like her. "Truth be told, and you've probably already heard this, but we started an online company that chases down predators before they can get to kids. We caught one just the other day."

She tried not to sound too proud, but frankly, she was. They'd worked hard to catch that asshole, and now he was in prison.

"Excellent," Nia said. "I would like to get involved if possible." She frowned. "Although I know Leah is still playing hard to get for Jasper." She tossed her purse toward the sofa. "It is a lot of fun to watch, just so you know."

Ivy could only look at the woman, not sure what to say. Athan's grams was much different than she'd expected, and she felt like she'd found an ally. Maybe even a friend. Her phone buzzed, and she pulled it from her pocket to read the screen. "Oh, no," she said.

"What is it?" Nia asked, leaning over.

Ivy looked toward the door and then back at the phone. "It's Leah. She found the main guy we've been trying to get, and he's arranged for a meet later." She bit her lip. There's no way Athan would let her go.

Nia quickly zipped up her coat. "Well, then, let's go help her out."

Ivy frowned. "I'm not sure how long Athan will be gone."

Nia retrieved her purse. "It sounds like they were headed to torture and interrogate somebody, and that has to do with Baston, the moron who's been chasing me through time. They won't be back for a few hours." Her voice remained cheerful, even as she discussed torture. She waved her hand dismissively in the air. "It's nothing we need to worry about right now. However, you know what this means?"

Ivy took a step back. "It means that I can go and help Leah, and you can stay safely here."

Nia threw back her head and laughed. "There are two guards on the elevator doors on the parking level. Honey, you're going to need my help getting by them."

Chapter Twelve

Oh, this was most definitely a mistake. Ivy knew it the second they reached the dilapidated motel on the far side of town. There was no coincidence that BlueEyes237 and Harry, the pervert they'd just caught, lived and operated out of the same town. She and Leah had been tracking these jerks for almost three months, and they had a nice little gang going in the large city of Buffalo. She was happy to be taking them down, but she should not have brought Athan's grandmother with her.

Nia, who had insisted upon driving, stopped the stolen SUV around the corner from the motel. The woman had been surprisingly quick about the theft. She'd also knocked out two of the guards at the elevator without much effort. Of course, they hadn't been expecting it, so they shouldn't be blamed.

Ivy shook her head. "You really shouldn't have knocked those guys out."

"Oh, they're fine," Nia said. "They're immortal. They'll be embarrassed, but they'll survive."

Ivy had no doubt Athan would be furious that she'd left to go meet Leah again. But considering she'd brought his grandmother, yeah, she might as well go on the run like Leah.

Nia reached out and patted her hand. "Stop worrying so much. We're doing something good, right?"

Ivy scratched her chin as the silence surrounded them. It was starting to get dark, and they would need to move inside soon. "Aren't you a little bit worried about your husband? The one thing they asked us to do was stay safe."

Nia laughed. "I've been mated for three millennia. Safety is an illusion, but it's nice that you still have it." She opened the door and jumped out of the vehicle. "Come on, let's go see Leah."

Thunder rolled high above, and a light rain pattered as they ran across the parking lot and around the corner toward door number twelve.

Ivy knocked quickly, and Leah opened it. Her eyes widened when she saw Nia. "Grams," she said, pulling her in for a hug. "It's so good to see you." She looked out at the darkness and tugged both women into the motel room. "What in the world are you doing here?"

Ivy blinked, surprised. She had expected anything but joy from her old friend.

Nia laughed and hugged her again. "Oh, I was finally meeting Ivy, and she received your text, so I thought I'd come help."

"That's fantastic," Leah said, grinning. "I missed you so much."

Nia nodded. "I know. I miss you, too, but there's no question they've been watching me just in case I caught up with you." She hip-checked Leah. "When are you going to stop running that boy in circles?"

Leah frowned. "I'm not running him in circles. I just…it didn't work, Nia. *We* didn't work."

Nia rolled her stunning eyes. "Oh, please. You're just being stubborn, and so is he. But he will catch you at some point. You know that, right?"

Leah grinned, and a dimple winked in her left cheek. "Maybe, maybe not. I've gotten pretty good at this thing."

"Huh," Nia said. "You kids, you never learn." Then she looked around the dusty motel room. "This place smells like cat urine."

"I think it is cat pee," Leah agreed.

This was even worse than the last cheap motel Ivy had been in. This one had a double bed with a dirty gray bedspread, a purple shag carpet, and walls that were so dirty they appeared yellow when they were supposed to be white. A film of dust and yellow pollen covered every surface. A rickety dresser and a dented bedside table were the only furniture in the room besides the bed. Leah's laptop lay open on the mattress.

"How did you get ahold of him finally?" Ivy asked.

Leah shrugged. "I just kept getting on the internet and he said he wanted to meet. I think he's worried about his friend. Good ole Harry got arrested, remember?"

"Oh," Ivy said, her shoulders settling. "That makes sense. So, we're expecting a trap?"

"Oh, we're definitely expecting a trap," Leah said. "I haven't sent him the address yet, but we need to be ready as soon as I do. I have weapons in the closet."

"I'm ready for this," Ivy said.

The door burst open, and a large man filled it with a semiautomatic weapon in his hand. "I'm ready, too." He looked around, studied the three of them, and then slowly stepped all the way inside before shutting the door. "Where's Harry, and what did he tell you?"

Ivy couldn't breathe. She took two steps to the side as Nia went the other way, leaving Leah in the middle. If he fired, he could only shoot one of them, and the other two could rush him. As a human, he was a good size, over six feet and solid muscle, and he had to be in his early fifties. The jerk looked like he could fight. His eyes were green, though.

"You're BlueEyes237?" Leah settled her stance.

"That's me," he said. "I know who you are, and I know you entrapped Harry. What I want to know is what he told you."

Oh, man, he thought they were private detectives or something like that. Ivy cut a look at Leah, and she gave a barely perceptible nod.

"Why don't you tell us everything and we'll say you cooperated," Ivy said evenly, trying to sound authoritative.

"How about you tell me everything and I don't shoot your ass?" the guy said.

"How'd you find us?" Leah asked.

The guy looked around the crappy motel room. "You're not the only one who can track an IP address. The Wi-Fi here isn't secure."

Leah frowned. "I guess I got a little too excited to finally meet you, *not* blue eyes. Who are you anyway?"

"That's a question you'll never have answered."

Vehicles roared into the lot outside, tires screeching wildly as they slammed on their brakes.

"Dammit," the man yelled, pivoting. "You set me up."

"Of course, we set you up," Leah said, frowning. "But I actually don't know who's out there." She edged to the gross-looking red velvet curtains and peered outside. "Uh-oh. This is so bad."

"What?" Nia asked, hurrying toward the window.

"Hey," the man yelled. "I'm the one with a gun."

"Just a second," Ivy said, holding up a finger and hurrying to the other side, looking outside. Did Athan find us?"

"No," Leah said, paling. "That isn't Athan out there."

Ivy gulped and opened the curtain wider to see Kurjan soldiers stepping out of the two nearest SUVs. They were easy to recognize from Athan's description of them. Everything inside her went cold. She looked toward the bathroom. "Is there a window there we can use to get out?"

"I think so—" Leah started to say.

Just then, projectiles flew through the window, shattering the glass and spinning in every direction. Smoke started to pour through the room, and then the floor seemed to explode.

* * * *

Fear was a new feeling for Athan, one he couldn't quite grasp as he tunneled through the streets of Buffalo in the SUV, careening around other cars and pushing the vehicle to its limit. "I can't believe it," he muttered.

His grandfather looked out the window, his gun at the ready, his body tense. "Agreed."

Athan took a sharp left as the storm increased in force, and he had to flip on the windshield wipers. "There was one exit. It was an elevator on the parking level."

"I'm aware," his grandfather said, glancing at his phone. "Take the next right."

"We had guards stationed at the elevator," Athan muttered. "Good ones. Protective ones. They should have been safe."

"They were safe. Next left."

Athan jerked the wheel sharply to the left. "I can't believe they knocked out the guards."

His grandfather sighed. "Me, either. I have to admit, I thought we left them secure. Next right."

Athan yanked the wheel to the right and then glanced at his grandfather. "Aren't you angry?"

"Sure. Next left."

Athan shook his head. It was one thing for Ivy and Leah to go off into danger, but to involve his grandmother? It was just too much. "I'm sorry about this, Gramps."

His grandfather looked over, surprise in his blue eyes. "What do you mean? It was your grandmother who knocked out the guards." He watched the screen. "I have to admit, I wasn't expecting her to do something like that now that we're back at war. Last year, sure. But I don't think she realizes the danger she's in."

Athan shook his head and punched the gas even harder. "I don't think either of them realizes the danger they're in."

"You haven't even met Baston," Cathal murmured. "I really do need to kill that asshole."

While Athan hadn't met Baston, he had been trained since the time he could walk to know that the Kurjan was their enemy and he'd come after them someday. The day had come. "Apparently, I haven't explained things well enough to Ivy."

"We'll get them back, and you can explain things later." His grandfather rubbed the whiskers along his hard jaw. "You know they went to meet Leah. Maybe it's time we brought her back into the fold. I know Jasper would appreciate it."

"Oh, that's definitely the plan." Athan shook his head. "I honestly thought that after last night, Ivy would be more..." He had to turn the windshield wipers up higher.

His grandfather threw back his head and laughed. "More what? Agreeable? Pliable? Submissive?"

"Well, yeah," Athan muttered.

His grandfather laughed harder. "I've been mated for thirty years shy of three thousand years. They don't get more pliable through the millennia, son. Believe me."

"That's probably why you have a tracker on Grams," Athan muttered, taking the next left.

His grandfather snorted. "That's exactly why I have a tracker on her. Funny thing is, she has no idea."

"She's about to," Athan said. A wave of electricity hit him, and he eased up on the gas, his senses flaring. "Did you get that?"

"Yeah. Pull over."

Athan rolled to a stop beneath several worn and tired-looking trees, all missing their leaves. What a depressing place. "How far are we?"

"We're less than a mile."

Panic tried to take hold, and Athan shoved it down, going stone-cold. "I sense at least three Kurjans."

"Me, too." Cathal lost the lazy indulgence in his eyes now that he'd also scented the Kurjans. "This was funny when we were just dealing with humans. Now, it's serious. Those two never should've left safety."

"Are the Kurjans on us, or have we come upon them?" Athan asked.

His grandfather paused and shut his eyes as if reaching out. "I can't tell."

"Me, either," Athan said, jumping out of the vehicle and tucking his gun into his waistband. "Let's assume the worst."

His grandpa jumped out and strapped a gun to his thigh. At three thousand years old, Cathal Maxwell looked every inch the warrior he'd always been. Experience had been stamped hard on his features, and as he prepared for battle, his eyes morphed to a startling copper.

Athan turned and sprinted through the rain, heading toward what appeared to be a one-story building. An explosion ripped through the night, and they both paused. "Shit," he muttered, ducking his head and launching into a full-out run.

Cathal followed suit, and they passed several sad and dreary apartment buildings before coming close to what appeared to be a motel that looked like it should be shut down. Several new SUVs idled in the parking lot, and smoke poured from one of the rooms.

"I'll go left," Athan said.

His grandfather nodded and moved to the right, both using the rain and the SUVs as cover. Athan reached the nearest one and found it empty. So, the Kurjans hadn't had much time to prepare for this. He watched as a tall Kurjan soldier, skin luminous in the storm, pulled Leah and Ivy out of the room. They were both bent over and coughing as smoke surrounded them. Another Kurjan brought his grandmother, and a third brought a sniveling human who looked like he'd had his nose broken.

Athan crept closer. The nearest Kurjan lifted his head as if catching a scent. The storm had masked Athan just long enough. He leaped forward, shoved Ivy and Leah out of the way, and punched the Kurjan in the throat while his grandfather went for the second one.

The Kurjan in front of Athan leaned back, reached for his weapon, and Athan yanked his knife from his boot and stabbed him, taking him down to the ground and embedding the knife through his throat into the chipped concrete.

The third Kurjan leaped for him and caught him in a tackle, and they rolled end over end across the sharp and jagged concrete littered with glass. Pain flared in Athan's neck, and he flipped them over, quickly knocking the younger soldier out with three sharp blows to the temple. The Kurjan struggled, and a pin dropped to the ground before a grenade rolled out of his pocket.

"Shit," Athan muttered, falling to the side and grasping the soldier's shirt to yank him up. The grenade exploded, throwing the guy into Athan and knocking them both back several yards to hit and dent the SUV. The Kurjan fell unconscious.

Athan's ears rang, and he shoved the body off him, staggering to his feet. He glanced over to see his grandfather straightening and looking almost bored with a prone Kurjan at his feet.

"It was a new squad, and they were young," Athan said, looking around.

His grandfather nodded. "Yeah. They must have been called in at the last second. Reinforcements should be coming soon."

Athan stumbled toward his mate, who was staring wide-eyed at the three Kurjans on the ground. "We have to go." He looked around. "Where is Leah?" The woman was nowhere to be seen.

"Damn it," his grandfather muttered.

Chapter Thirteen

Everything hurt. Ivy lay still in the luxurious leather recliner and experienced the oddest sensation of healing cells popping over her body. It was intriguing, even though her head felt like it had taken the full brunt of the explosion. Who would've expected they had grenades? Perhaps she and Leah had been in over their heads a little bit, but how could they have known the Kurjans would show up?

The private jet was smooth through the sky and oddly quiet. She opened her eyelids to see Athan sitting across from her in a chair with the wounds down the side of his face slowly mending. While his body looked relaxed, lounged in the matching chair, and his expression was calm, his eyes were anything but. The blues in his irises almost morphed to a pure golden color this time, and it wasn't a pretty mellow gold. This was fierce and sharp and aimed at her.

She winced. "Sorry I got you blown up."

A cut along his collarbone slowly mended. "You went in there without two thoughts, Ivy," he murmured. "That's not acceptable."

She'd had a job to do, and she'd thought she had a good plan. Apparently, not. "You know what we were doing?" She wondered how to fix her wrist, which was still sending out echoes of pain. It was a pretty good bruise and a possible sprain, and she needed to fix it before the next campaign.

"I think I have the gist," he said. "But you didn't plan as you should have, and taking my grams wasn't wise."

She threw up her hands. "We've been planning this for months, and I tried to stop her."

"How did that turn out?" he asked quietly.

That was a good point and one she didn't want to admit. "Even so." Irritation started to filter through the pain in her neck. "It would've turned out a lot better if the war between your family and the Kurjans hadn't interfered," she retorted. "You do realize that part of the reason this op went bad was because of you."

"This op?" he murmured. "You went from running a successful farm-friendly business to running ops?" His eyes flashed a heated blue. "I don't think so."

She wasn't going to sit in a posh plane and fight with him about it. She'd gotten away from him once, and she could do it again. "We closed down that entire internet ring, and we'd do it again." They had already confirmed that BlueEyes was in police headquarters, babbling a mile a minute about all his pervert friends. It was a success as far as she was concerned. "We'll do better next time."

"No next time." A cut along his ear slowly mended. His phone dinged, and he lifted it from the table to read the screen. Then he eased it back down.

"What?" she asked.

He drew air in through his nose and exhaled slowly. "My grandfather questioned the Kurjan we took with us, and they have a line on you."

She gulped. "How?"

"Don't know. But when they fired upon my car the other day, they were aiming for you. You're a target because they know about us, and it's a way to take me out." He shook his head. "They didn't even know it was my car—just that you had a funeral and were in it."

So, they'd tried to kill her. She swallowed. "How did they find me?"

"You haven't been all that private with your different jobs and lives and funerals. While we don't know how they found you, we know that they did. The soldier my grandfather is questioning is low level and won't have many more answers."

She'd have to be more careful in the future. She looked around. While she'd flown private several times, she hadn't seen a plane quite this nice. It was obvious the Maxwell clan had resources she hadn't quite realized.

The interior was wide, with leather chairs on either side of a rather spacious aisle. A large screen hung on the bulkhead. There was a bedroom in the back, and the two pilots were shut away by a heavy oak door.

"Where are we going?" she asked, trying not to sound as irritated as she felt.

He hadn't told her anything after loading her up in the car and then the plane.

"We're headed to our family's headquarters," he murmured.

Her chin lowered. "And that would be where?"

"That will be something you'll find out when we get there."

She glared at him. "I can't believe you don't trust me after all this time."

A flash of surprise quickly crossed his face, only to be blanked almost immediately. "You shot me." A threat of anger still rode his words. "Then you defied me and left the safety of the penthouse with my grandmother."

She winced. "Yeah, but I had to help Leah. Besides, you're immortal, so shooting you doesn't really count."

In addition, now that they had finally mated completely, he could obviously heal himself much faster than he had before.

Her wounds were also healing quicker, which would probably be handy if she continued screwing up ops like she just had. "Athan, we're going to have to get a couple of things straight."

"Oh, baby," he murmured, "believe me, we are going to get a couple of things straight." His voice was a low grumble. "We're mated. Things changed."

Irritation clawed at her. "So, you thought we'd mate, and I'd just fall in line? Have freedom for years and...what? Say, '*thanks*?'"

He cocked his head. "Something like that. Now, come here."

Not a chance. Not in a million years. She swallowed and wondered how close they were to the ground. Was it possible they were descending? "No."

One of his dark eyebrows rose, giving him the look of a hungry predator. "You don't want me to tell you again."

True. Very true. She didn't want to hear another word from him. But she couldn't stay there and win a staring contest, so she bunched her muscles and leaped up, aiming for the bedroom.

She didn't make it.

* * * *

Athan snagged her around the waist and took her to the plush carpet. She landed beneath him, and he stretched out, grasping her wrists and holding them over her head. She struggled against him and then laughed, the sound free and wild.

God. He loved her laugh. Desire filtered through her eyes, and a blush covered her Irish rose face. Still, she struggled.

He had to admire that. "No putting yourself in danger," he said, leaning down and kissing her. Hard.

She kissed him back and lifted her legs, settling her knees against his flanks and allowing her small body to cradle his erect cock. "I didn't put myself in danger. The danger came with you."

She wasn't wrong. Danger did come with him, but now, so did she. He kissed her again, letting his body take over.

Her fingers curled over his hands, and she dug her nails into his skin.

He lifted up. "The Kurjans have a line on you, and we have to be more careful, Ivy." He couldn't lose her now. He loved her more than he ever thought he could love anybody, and it had been hell staying away from her for years.

Of course, she'd been correct in that he had thought she'd just fall in line. Apparently, the freedom she'd enjoyed had allowed her to learn her strength, and the woman was strong. He could see it in her, and it made him want her more. Even so, she was his, and she needed to know that fact.

So, he released her hands and rolled until she was on top of him, tearing off her shirt in the process. She gasped and planted her hands on his pecs, leaning over. Her fall of silky hair brushed his cheek when she leaned down and nipped his nose.

"I can be more careful if you can," she murmured.

"Oh, you're definitely gonna be more careful." He reached up and released her bra. Fire, need, and heat flashed through him so quickly his ears heated. Then he traced her skin with his fingers, tapping up to the bite mark on her neck.

She shuddered, and her eyes darkened. Yeah, they would always have this.

Scrambling, she reached down and pulled his shirt up and then murmured as she leaned down and kissed his chest. He let her play for a while and then removed the rest of their clothing, rolling over until she was once again beneath him.

"When I tell you to stay somewhere, you need to do it."

She bit his chest and then ran her nails down his flanks to dig into his butt. "I'll do what I want. We both know it."

Oh, she was definitely a Maxwell mate. There was no doubt about that. He moved to the side and lifted her, planting her squarely across his knees.

She yelped and then laughed out loud. "Not again. We're in the plane."

He smacked her, smiling.

"Damn it, Athan." She laughed again. "You have got to stop this."

"No, you need to stop putting yourself in danger." Although her exhilaration and bravery were impressive, he really did need to keep her alive. It was good that he could have fun and laugh with her when it came to this. She did need to submit, and she needed to learn that. He smacked her several times until she started to squirm. "I understand that you want to make a difference in this world, and I'm more than happy to help you do that."

"I'll make a difference by taking off your head," she snapped.

Humor bubbled through him as he rubbed her reddened flesh. "The bottom line is, you have to stay safe."

"So you can live," she muttered, her voice muffled.

He lifted her then so she straddled him with his back against the wall of the plane. "No, so you can live. I love you. Don't you know that?"

She blinked, and her mouth fell open. "No, you never said it."

Now, he had. "Well, I do. You're everything." That was it. He had no more to give. She was everything.

She leaned in and kissed him. "I love you, too. I've loved you forever."

Until right that second, he hadn't realized how much he'd needed to hear those words. He tangled his fingers in her hair and yanked her head back. Then he leaned in and kissed her, giving her everything that he'd ever be. He had no doubt they'd have plenty of arguments throughout the years, but if his grandparents could make it century upon century, so could they.

He planted them both on the carpet and slowly entered her. Finally coming home.

She wrapped around him and then kissed him again. "You know it's going to be a wild ride, right?"

"I know," he said, kissing her deeply. "I've always known."

Epilogue

Montana was stunning this time of year. Ivy turned her face up to the sun and admired the beautiful fall foliage. Red, gold, orange…and every shade of yellow burst wildly in the trees around her. The Maxwell ranch was located against the Crazy Mountain Range, and apparently, her mate owned one of the many sprawling log homes scattered around the hundred thousand acres.

Surely, it was a coincidence, yet Ivy had to admit that if anybody belonged in the Crazy Mountains, it was the Maxwell clan.

In all of her years, she'd never lived on a ranch. There were working horses, cattle, and dogs. She'd already used her enhancement several times to see what they needed, and for the most part, they were healthy and content. One of the herding dogs had felt lonely, so she found a match for him online, and his new friend should arrive in a day or so.

She rocked in contentment in the carved chair on the wide deck, noting several deer in the area. One nodded at her and then scampered off.

Ivy watched as Klyde meandered through the trees and approached her, two mugs in his hands. "Try these." His jaw was bruised as if he'd been in a fight.

"What happened to your face?"

"Disagreement about recipes," he said easily.

She dutifully took both mugs by the handles. "Um, are you still mad at me for shooting you in the chest?" It was a fair question, and she wanted an answer before she sipped anything.

The youngest Maxwell brother leaned against a rough wooden pillar, his lips tipping into a grin. "Of course not. If I didn't get shot by a family member once in a while, I'd worry I wasn't needed any longer."

Yep. The Maxwells were unique.

"Maybe your mate will shoot you, as well," Ivy suggested.

"She wouldn't dare, whoever she is," he said, losing the humor glimmering in his eyes. "While it's fine if my sisters shoot me, my mate will behave once I find her. Period."

Interesting. Now Ivy wanted to shoot him again. She looked down at the two steaming mugs. One red, one blue…both heavy and ceramic. "Want one?"

"No." Klyde's black hair was windswept, and his tawny eyes sparkling. "I want you to taste both and say which one is better."

She sighed. While she'd only been on the ranch for a week, she'd already learned that the six brothers were impossibly competitive. The oldest, Raine, was due home in a day, and she'd heard he was worse than the rest, which was impossible as far as she was concerned. "Fine." She sipped delicately from the red cup and then gasped, her eyes filling with tears. Fire burned down her throat. "What is that?" She coughed.

"Moonshine," Nia said, striding out of the woods. She wore black jeans, a fall-themed green sweater, and a sweet smile. "Klyde and Collin compete every year."

It tasted more like antifreeze. Ivy sniffed and took a very small drink from the blue cup. The liquid burned her tongue until she wasn't sure it'd ever work again. She cleared her throat. "They're both terrible. Absolutely horrible."

Nia laughed. "Klyde? Back to the drawing board."

Klyde frowned, reclaimed the mugs, and turned toward the trail between the trees. "Huh. I need more cinnamon." He strode away, still mumbling to himself.

Nia shook her head and settled her spectacular brown boots more securely on the dying leaves. "Good answer. Also, I heard from Leah. She's moved on from Tennessee. Wouldn't tell me where."

Ivy kept rocking. "I'm not surprised." Although she was sorry she wouldn't be able to continue their work.

"Jasper seems to be on a mission." Nia's eyes sparkled. "I think Leah will be home soon. For now, I thought you and I could continue your campaigns from that business you set up. I'd like to keep getting jerks locked up."

Ivy perked up. "Me, too."

"Good." Nia glanced behind her. "I have a secure computer room in my basement. Let's meet there after dinner."

Athan moved into view from the trail and paused. "Grams? What's up? I thought you were getting ready for the barbecue."

Nia patted his arm. "Don't be late." She winked at Ivy and then turned down the trail.

Ivy studied her mate, her entire body short-circuiting. Every time he was near, she felt electrified. Alive and powerful. "Hi."

He looked her over from head to toe, his glittering blue gaze taking all of her in. "Whatever you and my grams are planning, stop it."

"Sure," Ivy said easily. "But we're not planning anything." How odd that she'd found not only a kindred spirit but also a friend in her mate's grandmother. What a wonderful world she'd entered.

"Humph," he grumbled, the sun glinting off his dark hair and highlighting the powerful angles in his handsome face.

Her body warmed. "We have a few minutes before the barbecue." She loved having a family.

"Right. I wanted to warn you." He straightened, looking even more powerful against the wild forest. "Jasper is on a tear to find Leah. He's going to ask you questions, but don't worry, I'll be there."

Amusement tickled through her. "I'm not afraid of your brother."

"Good." Athan stalked toward her and made quick use of the three steps to the deck. "You're not afraid of much."

No, she really wasn't. She was finally right where she belonged: with her mate and her new family. There were fun times ahead, and she'd make a difference where she could. She and Nia would do that, and Leah could join in whenever she decided to come home. "I like our home," Ivy murmured.

His eyes flared. "Let's make good use of it. We do have a few minutes." He paused, the sun lighting him from behind, his eyes still glowing. The male was everything she could've ever wanted...and more.

She blinked sudden tears from her eyes. "I love you, Athan Maxwell."

His chin lifted. Tension, the good kind, rolled from him. "I love *you*, mate."

Her heart jumped and then settled. "Prove it."

He moved faster than was possible, scooping her from the chair and striding into the cabin. "I will. Every day into forever."

* * * *

Also from 1001 Dark Nights and Rebecca Zanetti, discover Vampire, Vixen, Vengeance, Blaze Erupting, Tangled, Teased, and Tricked.

Sign up for the 1001 Dark Nights Newsletter
and be entered to win a Tiffany Key necklace.

There's a contest every month!

Go to www.1001DarkNights.com to subscribe.

**As a bonus, all subscribers can download
FIVE FREE exclusive books!**

Discover 1001 Dark Nights Collection Ten

DRAGON LOVER by Donna Grant
A Dragon Kings Novella

KEEPING YOU by Aurora Rose Reynolds
An Until Him/Her Novella

HAPPILY EVER NEVER by Carrie Ann Ryan
A Montgomery Ink Legacy Novella

DESTINED FOR ME by Corinne Michaels
A Come Back for Me/Say You'll Stay Crossover

MADAM ALANA by Audrey Carlan
A Marriage Auction Novella

DIRTY FILTHY BILLIONAIRE by Laurelin Paige
A Dirty Universe Novella

HIDE AND SEEK by Laura Kaye
A Blasphemy Novella

TANGLED WITH YOU by J. Kenner
A Stark Security Novella

TEMPTED by Lexi Blake
A Masters and Mercenaries Novella

THE DANDELION DIARY by Devney Perry
A Maysen Jar Novella

CHERRY LANE by Kristen Proby
A Huckleberry Bay Novella

THE GRAVE ROBBER by Darynda Jones
A Charley Davidson Novella

CRY OF THE BANSHEE by Heather Graham
A Krewe of Hunters Novella

DARKEST NEED by Rachel Van Dyken
A Dark Ones Novella

CHRISTMAS IN CAPE MAY by Jennifer Probst
A Sunshine Sisters Novella

A VAMPIRE'S MATE by Rebecca Zanetti
A Dark Protectors/Rebels Novella

WHERE IT BEGINS by Helena Hunting
A Pucked Novella

Also from Blue Box Press

THE MARRIAGE AUCTION by Audrey Carlan
Season One, Volume One
Season One, Volume Two
Season One, Volume Three
Season One, Volume Four

THE JEWELER OF STOLEN DREAMS by M.J. Rose

LOVE ON THE BYLINE by Xio Axelrod
A Plays and Players Novel

SAPPHIRE STORM by Christopher Rice writing as C. Travis Rice
A Sapphire Cove Novel

ATLAS: THE STORY OF PA SALT by Lucinda Riley and Harry
Whittaker

A SOUL OF ASH AND BLOOD by Jennifer L. Armentrout
A Blood and Ash Novel

Discover More Rebecca Zanetti

Vampire
A Dark Protectors/Rebels Novella

Dr. Mariana Lopez has finally stopped bailing friends out of difficult situations. Well, except for substituting as the leader for another anger management group, pitching in as a campaign strategist for a prospective sheriff, and babysitting three dogs. Even with such a full life, she can feel the danger around her—a sense that something isn't right. Nightmares harass her, until the real thing comes to life, and only the dark and sexy male sitting in her group can save her. However, with safety comes a price she might not be willing to pay.

Raine Maxwell is one of the Maxwells out of Montana, which means he's not only one of the most deadly vampires alive, but his path is set and his mate has been chosen for him. To save him—to continue his line. Unfortunately, his mate is an enhanced human female who has no idea of her abilities, of his species, or of her future. He'd like to lead her gently into this new world, but his people aren't the only ones who've found her, which puts her into more danger than she can imagine. Plus, in order to follow his laws, he only has one week to convince her that immortality with him is what she wants—and needs.

* * * *

Vixen
A Dark Protectors/Rebels Novella

Tabi Rusko has a simple to-do list: Rob a bank, steal a recording, set up a lucrative factory, and survive the assassins on her tail. Sure, she's a demoness with the cunning and instincts that come with her species, but she's always spent more time exploring than training, and her fighting skills are okay at best. One sexy man, a human cop no less, is responsible for her being stuck in a small hick town and forced into a human anger-management group that's crazier than her. To make matters worse, his dangerous blue eyes and hard body leave her breathless and ready to rumble, and his overbearing attitude is a challenge a demoness can't refuse.

Evan O'Connell just wants to enjoy his time out of the military by policing a small town and hopefully pulling cats from trees and helping old ladies cross the street before he succumbs to the disease plaguing him. The last thing he needs is a stunning, too sexy, pain in the butt blonde casing his bank and causing a ruckus everywhere she goes. There's something different about her that he can't figure out, and when she offers him immortality in exchange for her freedom, he discovers that isn't enough. One touch of her, a whirlwind beyond his imagination, and he wants the Vixen to be his forever, as soon as he takes care of the centuries-old killers on her tail.

* * * *

Vengeance
A Dark Protectors/Rebels Novella

Vengeance and revenge are the only forces driving vampire soldier Noah Siosal since losing his brother to an enemy he's been unable to find. He's searched every corner of the globe, going through adversaries and piling up bodies until finally getting a lead. The last place he wants to be is in a ridiculous anger management group with people expressing feelings instead of taking action. Until one fragile human, a green-eyed sweetheart being stalked by danger, catches his eye. One touch, and he realizes vengeance can't be anywhere near her.

Anger and self-preservation are the only motivations Abby Miller needs or wants right now. Falsely accused of attacking the man who's terrorized her for years, she's forced as a plea bargain to attend an anger management counseling group with people with some serious rage issues, while learning true self-defense on the side. Yet a man, one more primal than any she's ever met, draws her in a way and into a world deadlier than she's ever imagined. He offers her protection, but she finds the fight is really for his heart, and she's ready to battle.

* * * *

Blaze Erupting
Scorpius Syndrome/A Brigade Novella

Hugh Johnson is nobody's hero, and the idea of being in the

limelight makes him want to growl. He takes care of his brothers, does his job, and enjoys a mellow evening hanging with his hound dog and watching the sports channel. So when sweet and sexy Ellie Smithers from his college chemistry class asks him to save millions of people from a nuclear meltdown, he doggedly steps forward while telling himself that the world hasn't changed and he can go back to his relaxing life. One look at Ellie and excitement doesn't seem so bad.

Eleanor Smithers knows that the Scorpius bacteria has and will change life as we know it, but that's a concern for another day. She's been hand-picked as the computer guru for The Brigade, which is the USA's first line of defense against all things Scorpius, including homegrown terrorists who've just been waiting for a chance to strike. Their target is a nuclear power plant in the east, and the only person who can help her is Hugh, the sexy, laconic, dangerous man she had a crush on so long ago.

* * * *

Tangled
A Dark Protectors—Reece Family Novella

Now that her mask has finally slipped…

Ginny O'Toole has spent a lifetime repaying her family's debt, and she's finally at the end of her servitude with one last job. Of course, it couldn't be easy. After stealing the computer files that will free her once and for all, she finds herself on the run from a pissed-off vampire who has never fallen for her helpless act. A deadly predator too sexy for his own good. If he doesn't knock it off, he's going to see just how powerful she can really be.

He won't be satisfied until she's completely bare.

Theo Reese had been more than irritated at the beautiful yet helpless witch he'd known a century ago, thinking she was just useless fluff who enjoyed messing with men's heads. The second he discovers she's a ruthless thief determined to bring down his family, his blood burns and his interest peaks, sending his true nature into hunting mode. When he finds her, and he will, she'll understand the real meaning of helpless.

****

Tricked
A Dark Protectors—Reese Family Novella

He Might Save Her

Former police psychologist Ronni Alexander had it all before a poison attacked her heart and gave her a death sentence. Now, on her last leg, she has an opportunity to live if she mates a vampire. A real vampire. One night of sex and a good bite, and she'd live forever with no more weaknesses. Well, except for the vampire whose dominance is over the top, and who has no clue how to deal with a modern woman who can take care of herself.

She Might Kill Him

Jared Reese, who has no intention of ever mating for anything other than convenience, agrees to help out his new sister-in-law by saving her friend's life with a quick tussle in bed. The plan seems so simple. They'd mate, and he move on with his life and take risks as a modern pirate should. Except after one night with Ronni, one moment of her sighing his name, and he wants more than a mating of convenience. Now all he has to do is convince Ronni she wants the same thing. Good thing he's up for a good battle.

****

Teased
A Dark Protectors—Reece Family Novella

The Hunter

For almost a century, the Realm's most deadly assassin, Chalton Reese, has left war and death in the past, turning instead to strategy, reason, and technology. His fingers, still stained with blood, now protect with a keyboard instead of a weapon. Until the vampire king sends him on one more mission: to hunt down a human female with the knowledge to destroy the Realm. A woman with eyes like emeralds, a brain to match his own, and a passion that might destroy them both—if the enemy on their heels doesn't do so first.

The Hunted

Olivia Roberts has forgone relationships with wimpy metro-sexuals in favor of pursuing a good story, bound and determined to uncover the truth, any truth. When her instincts start humming about missing proprietary information, she has no idea her search for a story will lead her to a ripped, sexy, and dangerous male beyond any human man. Setting aside the unbelievable fact that he's a vampire and she's his prey, she discovers that trusting him is the only chance they have to survive the danger stalking them both.

About Rebecca Zanetti

New York Times, USA Today, Publisher's Weekly and *Wall Street Journal* bestselling author Rebecca Zanetti has published more than sixty novels, which have been translated into several languages, with millions of copies sold world-wide. Her books have received *Publisher's Weekly* and *Kirkus* starred reviews and have been featured in *Entertainment Weekly*, *Woman's World*, and *Women's Day* magazines. Her novels have also been included in Amazon best books of the year and have been favorably reviewed in both the *Washington Post* and the *New York Times* book reviews. Rebecca has ridden in a locked Chevy trunk, has asked the unfortunate delivery guy to release her from a set of handcuffs, and has discovered the best silver mine shafts in which to bury a body…all in the name of research. Honest. Find Rebecca at: www.RebeccaZanetti.com

Discover 1001 Dark Nights

by Rebecca Zanetti ~ DIRTY WICKED by Shayla Black ~ THE ONLY ONE by Lauren Blakely ~ SWEET SURRENDER by Liliana Hart

COLLECTION FOUR
ROCK CHICK REAWAKENING by Kristen Ashley ~ ADORING INK by Carrie Ann Ryan ~ SWEET RIVALRY by K. Bromberg ~ SHADE'S LADY by Joanna Wylde ~ RAZR by Larissa Ione ~ ARRANGED by Lexi Blake ~ TANGLED by Rebecca Zanetti ~ HOLD ME by J. Kenner ~ SOMEHOW, SOME WAY by Jennifer Probst ~ TOO CLOSE TO CALL by Tessa Bailey ~ HUNTED by Elisabeth Naughton ~ EYES ON YOU by Laura Kaye ~ BLADE by Alexandra Ivy/Laura Wright ~ DRAGON BURN by Donna Grant ~ TRIPPED OUT by Lorelei James ~ STUD FINDER by Lauren Blakely ~ MIDNIGHT UNLEASHED by Lara Adrian ~ HALLOW BE THE HAUNT by Heather Graham ~ DIRTY FILTHY FIX by Laurelin Paige ~ THE BED MATE by Kendall Ryan ~ NIGHT GAMES by CD Reiss ~ NO RESERVATIONS by Kristen Proby ~ DAWN OF SURRENDER by Liliana Hart

COLLECTION FIVE
BLAZE ERUPTING by Rebecca Zanetti ~ ROUGH RIDE by Kristen Ashley ~ HAWKYN by Larissa Ione ~ RIDE DIRTY by Laura Kaye ~ ROME'S CHANCE by Joanna Wylde ~ THE MARRIAGE ARRANGEMENT by Jennifer Probst ~ SURRENDER by Elisabeth Naughton ~ INKED NIGHTS by Carrie Ann Ryan ~ ENVY by Rachel Van Dyken ~ PROTECTED by Lexi Blake ~ THE PRINCE by Jennifer L. Armentrout ~ PLEASE ME by J. Kenner ~ WOUND TIGHT by Lorelei James ~ STRONG by Kylie Scott ~ DRAGON NIGHT by Donna Grant ~ TEMPTING BROOKE by Kristen Proby ~ HAUNTED BE THE HOLIDAYS by Heather Graham ~ CONTROL by K. Bromberg ~ HUNKY HEARTBREAKER by Kendall Ryan ~ THE DARKEST CAPTIVE by Gena Showalter

COLLECTION SIX
DRAGON CLAIMED by Donna Grant ~ ASHES TO INK by Carrie Ann Ryan ~ ENSNARED by Elisabeth Naughton ~ EVERMORE by Corinne Michaels ~ VENGEANCE by Rebecca Zanetti ~ ELI'S TRIUMPH by Joanna Wylde ~ CIPHER by Larissa Ione ~ RESCUING MACIE by Susan Stoker ~ ENCHANTED by Lexi Blake ~ TAKE THE

BRIDE by Carly Phillips ~ INDULGE ME by J. Kenner ~ THE KING by Jennifer L. Armentrout ~ QUIET MAN by Kristen Ashley ~ ABANDON by Rachel Van Dyken ~ THE OPEN DOOR by Laurelin Paige ~ CLOSER by Kylie Scott ~ SOMETHING JUST LIKE THIS by Jennifer Probst ~ BLOOD NIGHT by Heather Graham ~ TWIST OF FATE by Jill Shalvis ~ MORE THAN PLEASURE YOU by Shayla Black ~ WONDER WITH ME by Kristen Proby ~ THE DARKEST ASSASSIN by Gena Showalter

COLLECTION SEVEN
THE BISHOP by Skye Warren ~ TAKEN WITH YOU by Carrie Ann Ryan ~ DRAGON LOST by Donna Grant ~ SEXY LOVE by Carly Phillips ~ PROVOKE by Rachel Van Dyken ~ RAFE by Sawyer Bennett ~ THE NAUGHTY PRINCESS by Claire Contreras ~ THE GRAVEYARD SHIFT by Darynda Jones ~ CHARMED by Lexi Blake ~ SACRIFICE OF DARKNESS by Alexandra Ivy ~ THE QUEEN by Jen Armentrout ~ BEGIN AGAIN by Jennifer Probst ~ VIXEN by Rebecca Zanetti ~ SLASH by Laurelin Paige ~ THE DEAD HEAT OF SUMMER by Heather Graham ~ WILD FIRE by Kristen Ashley ~ MORE THAN PROTECT YOU by Shayla Black ~ LOVE SONG by Kylie Scott ~ CHERISH ME by J. Kenner ~ SHINE WITH ME by Kristen Proby

COLLECTION EIGHT
DRAGON REVEALED by Donna Grant ~ CAPTURED IN INK by Carrie Ann Ryan ~ SECURING JANE by Susan Stoker ~ WILD WIND by Kristen Ashley ~ DARE TO TEASE by Carly Phillips ~ VAMPIRE by Rebecca Zanetti ~ MAFIA KING by Rachel Van Dyken ~ THE GRAVEDIGGER'S SON by Darynda Jones ~ FINALE by Skye Warren ~ MEMORIES OF YOU by J. Kenner ~ SLAYED BY DARKNESS by Alexandra Ivy ~ TREASURED by Lexi Blake ~ THE DAREDEVIL by Dylan Allen ~ BOND OF DESTINY by Larissa Ione ~ MORE THAN POSSESS YOU by Shayla Black ~ HAUNTED HOUSE by Heather Graham ~ MAN FOR ME by Laurelin Paige ~ THE RHYTHM METHOD by Kylie Scott ~ JONAH BENNETT by Tijan ~ CHANGE WITH ME by Kristen Proby ~ THE DARKEST DESTINY by Gena Showalter

On Behalf of 1001 Dark Nights,

Liz Berry, M.J. Rose, and Jillian Stein would like to thank ~

Steve Berry
Doug Scofield
Benjamin Stein
Kim Guidroz
Tanaka Kangara
Asha Hossain
Chris Graham
Chelle Olson
Kasi Alexander
Jessica Saunders
Dylan Stockton
Richard Blake
and Simon Lipskar

Printed in Great Britain
by Amazon